Indulgence

Caitlyn Black

DellArte
PRESS

Dellarte Press books may be ordered through booksellers or by contacting:

Dellarte Press™
1663 Liberty Drive
Bloomington, IN 47403
www.dellartepress.com
1-877-217-3420

ISBN: 978-1-4501-0021-2 (sc)
ISBN: 978-1-4501-0022-9 (e)

Printed in the United States of America

Dellarte Press rev. date: 08/21/2012

Table of Contents

Acknowledgements

First off, I would like to thank my wonderful children, Mark and Jordan. Without their love and light, nothing else would be possible. They encourage me to do my best every day of my life.

I would also like to acknowledge Pia Gabriela, my cover designer. She is beyond awesome. Her pictures go above and beyond my wildest imagination! Besides that, she is an amazing person and a very good friend.

Thank you to Paulette Kinnes, my editor. I can't even begin to tell you how much work she put into my manuscript. She gave me so many helpful hints about the story, as well as cleaning up my writing. If you enjoy this story, then you are seeing her fingerprint at work.

Masashi Kishimoto has been a major influence on my writing. I am a better person after reading his work. He has an amazing talent for writing characters that you can't help but fall in love with. Hopefully I was able to catch a fraction of that with my characters.

Lastly, I couldn't have finished this book without Rachel, my beta-reader. Her encouragement and helpful hints have been invaluable. She has stood by me during all the craziness. I appreciate it and will never forget her kindness and support.

Chapter 1

Interview

Thursday, August 16, 2012 - 3:15 p.m.

I landed the interview of a lifetime. I had been working in the banking and financial services industry since the age of 19, but this job was on a whole different level. I would be working for an Executive Director at one of the most prestigious firms in the country. The office resided in the heart of Manhattan, on the top floor of a 30-story building.

When the elevator doors opened, I noted with trepidation the glass doors enclosing the office. The large office covered half of the 30th floor. Inside, dark cherry-wood paneling embellished the walls, and the handcrafted black leather chairs and couches complemented those disturbingly expensive walls to perfection.

In the center of the enormous room sat a receptionist, who busied herself answering the numerous calls that rang in. She wore a professional business suit in a salmon color and petite tortoiseshell glasses that made her appear smart.

I peered down at my outfit one more time, hoping that my interview suit would suffice for the occasion. Then I shook it off.

No sense losing my confidence this early in the game.

I approached the reception desk. "I'm here to see Mr. Hardy."

The receptionist didn't even look up, rather, she pointed to the waiting area. "Please have a seat."

Dismissed by the receptionist. Not a good sign.

Nevertheless, I hesitantly sat down on the black leather couch. It was comfortable enough, but that didn't stop me from fidgeting. I crossed my legs and put my satchel on my lap. Then I held my hands together and fiddled with my fingers. I wanted to appear lady-like. But who was I kidding? I had never been lady-like before...

A few minutes later, another woman appeared. "He's ready to see you now."

This lady seemed to be another secretary. She was tall and blond, with her hair pulled back into a bun. I briefly wondered how many assistants this man had.

I couldn't tell if I felt relief that my wait was over or scared now that the time had arrived. Now my hands were sweating. How could I hide that? I would probably have to shake his hand. How embarrassing was this going to be?

The woman led me into a huge office with emerald green walls and furniture that matched the cherry-wood paneling in the outer office. A man was turned away from me behind the desk. It appeared that he was looking at the latest stock quotes on his computer screen.

Above his computer was a painting. But this painting didn't seem to be the normal stock picture that one would see hanging on a typical brokerage firm wall. It depicted a mother holding her toddler son on her lap. The boy had a dimpled smile and was reaching up to grab a tendril of his mother's ebony hair with his tiny hand. The woman gazed down at her son with radiant, dark-colored eyes.

The picture was an original. I could see the ridges of each color rising up against the canvas.

I then glanced at his desk. No personal pictures. But the desk was so humongous that the man sitting behind it looked small in comparison.

That is, until he turned around.

I immediately got lost in his liquid chocolate, almond-shaped eyes. And eerily enough, they matched the image of the young mother.

He was beautiful all around. His straight, silky jet-black hair fell to his shirt collar, and his flawless porcelain skin contrasted sharply with his dark hair and eyes. Through the black suit that he wore he appeared thin but well built.

"Ms. Jade, will you please have a seat." He stood momentarily and motioned to the black leather chair in front of his desk.

"That will be all, Ms. Swanson," he drawled with a smooth, textured voice.

The lady's name was apparently Ms. Swanson, because she exited the office and closed the door behind her.

I could hardly take my eyes off of him. When he stood, I could tell that he was tall, probably about six-foot-two. Since I'm five-foot-six, he would tower over me. For a boyfriend, that's kinda hot. But for a boss, maybe not so great...

He couldn't have been much older than me, but yet he was *this* successful. He must be really smart...or a very hard worker. Either way, I immediately liked him even more.

He sat back down in his own high-backed, black leather chair. He picked up my resume, which Ms. Swanson had left for him, and scanned it for details. I carefully studied his facial expressions as he read. I hoped that he would find something he liked.

His head didn't move, but his eyes found mine. "So you're registered to sell securities?"

"Yes sir, I am."

"Mmhmm." He grunted. "What makes you want to work here?"

Ack! Focus! Don't stare at the hot guy. Keep it together already!

"As you can see from my resume, I have been working my way up in the industry for eleven years. I believe that this opportunity is the logical next step in my career path."

"Textbook answer. Now, can you tell me the real reason?"

I froze. His eyes bore a hole in me. What was I supposed to say to that? *Think. Think!*

"Well, I like Manhattan, this company would be a good place to work, and I think this job has promotional opportunities."

"It doesn't. Now what?"

"What do you mean?"

"As my assistant, you would remain my assistant. What promotional opportunity is there in that?"

"I-I don't know?"

"Did you research this job at all before you came in here?"

"I-I guess not."

He pushed himself up from his chair, and I knew where this was going. I was done. I looked at him, with my mouth wide open and I'm sure a very sad look in my eyes.

"Please! Please give me a chance. I'm a hard worker, and I'm a quick learner. I know you'd be happy with me if you hired me."

Empathy showed through his eyes. "I'm sorry. But I don't think so."

"Why not? You don't even know me yet!"

"Do I want to get to know you?"

"Yes. Absolutely."

His tall, slim body descended back to his seat. "Then do it. Move me."

I sighed, but I knew that I wasn't out of the doghouse yet. What could I possibly do to change this man's mind about me? And how does one go about moving a man like this?

"I don't have all day." He swiveled his chair, and the blinking stock monitor showing on the computer screen regained his full attention.

"But sir, how can I have a conversation with you if you aren't even looking at me?"

"Do I *need* to look at you for some reason?"

"Yes."

"*Why?*"

"Because that's how people communicate. You know what? You're right. Maybe I'm not cut out for this job. I don't know how your other assistants deal with you!" I got up to leave, but that's when I heard the squeak of his chair as he turned around.

"They don't know how to deal with me either."

Wow. That was unexpected.

"I'm hard to work with. I admit it. And I just want someone who will be here long-term. I'm tired of having to hire new people all the time."

I sighed and returned to my seat. "Well sir, if you had taken the time to really look at my resume, you would have seen that I am pretty loyal. I stay at jobs much longer than most people do."

"Then why are you leaving your current position?"

"Okay, since you don't like textbook answers, how about this? My current boss is a total bitch. I don't think you're anything like her, so I think we'll get along fine."

"I love honesty."

"So I've gathered."

He quietly laughed. "You do pick things up pretty quickly. I like that. So let me ask you this. How do you feel about travel?"

"I love it."

"What if it's a lot of travel?"

"I love it even more."

"Don't you have anything keeping you home?" he inquired.

"Not a thing."

"That's sad."

"Not really."

A tiny smile crept onto his face. *Do I amuse him?* But there was something to that tiny smile. His full lips tugged upward slightly, and the smile never quite reached his eyes. It was somewhat unnerving. On the other hand, it showed the slightest touch of emotion from the man, and for that, I was grateful.

"Sir, may I ask *you* a question?"

"Sure."

"You obviously travel. How do *you* feel about it?"

"It's my job. I signed up for it. But I can assure you that it gets old after a while."

"That may be, but I think I can handle it for *quite* a while before that happens. So what will I be doing during all of this traveling?"

"Well you see, Ms. Jade, I have a full staff manning the office. The members of that staff handle my affairs while I'm gone. But I've never had anyone to help me on the road. There are lots of times that an assistant could help me prepare for presentations. I meet with clients out of town, and I also coordinate company-sponsored conferences for financial advisors around the country. I've always wanted someone to help me out. This position was created for that reason."

He paused, but then continued, "This position is for a glorified personal assistant. Basically, someone I can have at my beck and call. It isn't glamorous by any means. I wouldn't blame you if you turned it down."

It wasn't what I expected, but somehow, I was still intrigued.

He didn't say anything else. He just looked at me.

I fidgeted. His stare intensified my already heightened anxiety. "How often are you actually in the office?"

He thought about it. "About twenty-five percent of the time."

"So what do I do when we *aren't* on the road?"

"You are still at my beck and call."

I gasped.

His tiny smile returned. "If you're lucky enough to be in the office, then there would be travel arrangements to make, coordination of upcoming events, preparation for future client meetings. Don't worry. You *will* be busy."

"Um, how many assistants do you already have?"

"Four."

"And that isn't enough?"

"Not nearly."

"Why is that?"

"Whose interview is this, anyway?" he asked.

But I could tell that he was still amused. "If you come in on Monday, I will introduce you to everybody and let you know what each one does for me."

"Monday? You want me to be here on Monday?"

"Of course. I have a conference on Friday that I need you to get me ready for."

"But sir, I can't. I need to give my current employer two weeks' notice first."

"Whatever for?"

"It would be inconsiderate to leave her in a lurch like that."

"Do I care?"

"I do, and I don't want to burn a bridge. What if I need her as a reference someday?"

"Why would you? I told you that you will be my assistant from here on out. What do you need a reference for?"

Because you're a little crazy, and I can only stay as long as you remain sane. "It's always good to have a back-up plan, sir."

"Well, I'll leave it up to you. If you want the job, be here on Monday. If you want the reference, then stay there until you find a better offer." He turned his chair, and his focus went back to the flashing stock monitor.

I sat there for a second, staring at the back of his chair. *He can't be serious. Either come on Monday, or don't come at all? What kind of ultimatum is that?*

I stood, with my head held low, and slowly walked to the door. I blew it, and actually, the job did have its up sides. Travel with a hot-looking boss could be quite interesting. It certainly beat the heck out of answering phones for a raging bitch. Not to mention the sweet office in the middle of Manhattan. Plus, in my current job I was the only assistant for a female broker. I would be one of *five* assistants for an Executive Director! This sounded better and better.

I placed my hand on the doorknob and attempted to turn it. But it slipped right through my fingers. My hands had been sweating after all. I reached for it again, and this time a strong hand covered mine and helped me turn it.

"We start work at 8:00 a.m. on Monday. Pick up your offer letter at Ms. Swanson's desk on your way out." He breathed softly in my ear.

Mr. Hardy had surprised me from behind. I thought that he was still looking at stock quotes. *How did he get to the door so quickly? Is he some sort of ninja or something?*

His hand was warm to the touch, and due to his close proximity, I detected the scent of his cologne.

If I take this job, I'll have to get over this little crush that I have on him.

I peered at him and tried to smile. Due to his height, I had to tilt my head to gain eye contact. Big mistake. The obsidian orbs that I found gazing back at me almost knocked me off my feet.

With all the grace I could muster, I wobbled out of his office. All I could think was: *Don't trip! Don't make a fool of yourself in front of the hot guy!* I had worn high heels for the interview, but now I was convinced that I had made a big mistake. Walking a straight line would be impossible after that encounter!

He looked at me and gave me a small wave before closing his office door. I was relieved...at first. *Oh God, I should have asked him where Ms. Swanson sits before I left.* I looked around the office, and it was like a maze. I decided to go out the way that I had come in, and maybe I could ask the receptionist.

But she was on the phone.

After a minute of ignoring me, she shifted her eyes in my direction. "May I help you?"

"Where is Ms. Swanson's desk?"

She pointed her bony finger to the right corner of the office.

"Thank you." I traversed in that direction with a bounce in my step, being mindful of my high heels while doing it.

It was weird, but I *wanted* that offer letter. Then I could sleep on it and make my decision when I woke up in the morning.

The blond woman from earlier was busy typing something into her computer. When she noticed me coming toward her, she sighed. *Was that relief in her sigh?*

She smiled and stood. "Congratulations! I'm glad it worked out."

"Um, it hasn't worked out yet. I'm still deciding."

She raised her eyebrow at me. "I don't understand. Then why are you here for the letter?"

"Just in case."

"Well then," she turned toward her credenza and picked up a manila envelope, "here it is. I hope to see you on Monday."

I tried to smile, but I didn't know how to respond to that. "It was nice meeting you."

"Nice to meet you too."

I liked her. If I did take the job, I thought that I would enjoy getting to know her better.

I walked back up to the front of the office. There was that receptionist again. I didn't know if I wanted to say good-bye to her or stick my tongue out at her. I could already tell that she was a real peach.

Before I could decide, a large balding man stormed in through the glass doors and stomped up to her desk. "Get me Hardy. Now!"

"Y-yes, Mr. Biggerstaff."

She stutters? I never would have guessed. She scampered away from her desk like a mouse, in the direction of Mr. Hardy's office.

I had to admit that I was curious about what was happening. I sure hoped that it wouldn't affect my job offer. But it was awkward. So I silently opened the glass door and let myself out.

Chapter 2

First Day

Monday, August 20, 2012 - 7:30 a.m.

Well, there was nowhere else on Earth that I would rather have been than that Manhattan office at 7:30 a.m. the following Monday. I'm lying. I'd rather have been in bed! But it was much nicer than the office I had left last week. As could be expected, the psycho-bitch from hell was none too pleased at my announcement of immediate departure. But I didn't care. Let her answer her own damn phone!

It was early in the morning, and the elevators didn't work without a keycard. Luckily, Mr. Hardy had already put me on the list for the office, and the security guard let me in.

Mr. Hardy was pretty sure of himself. I never told him that I was coming.

I pushed the button for the 30th floor. Why was I feeling more nervous now than I had when I went up the elevator for the interview? I guess it was because I had nothing to lose at that point. Now I did. If he kicked me out today, I would have nowhere else to go. And my bills wouldn't pay themselves.

I heard the elevator chime, signaling that I had arrived at my floor. The elevator door opened, and I observed my new office. It was dark, and therefore nothing like its image from last week. I stepped up to open the glass door. Locked. *That figures.* I looked around to find a place to sit, but then, out of the corner of my eye, I saw a figure move inside. I knocked in an effort to get the person's attention. The vibration of the glass moving against the marble floor of the hallway caused a louder sound than my actual knock.

A young woman approached the glass door with a confused expression.

I shouted through the door, "My name's Katie Jade. I'm supposed to start work here today."

The woman nodded and turned the lock to let me in. She was beautiful. She had long, light brown hair and humongous crystal blue eyes. She was thin and about five feet tall. She appeared very professional-looking with her designer-made suit.

She smiled and extended her hand to me. "I'm Alyssa Gabrielle. Nice to meet you."

I shook her hand. It was a dainty handshake. I wasn't used to that. I could be kinda aggressive with my firm handshakes. I would have to take note of this.

"Is Mr. Hardy here?"

"Heck no!" She giggled. "He's never here until about 10:00."

"Oh, he told me to be here at 8:00."

She continued to giggle. "That's right. *You* need to be here at 8:00. He needs to be here whenever he feels like it."

"Oh..." *What do you say to that on your first day at a new job?*

She looked at me and asked, "Do you know your way around?"

"Not really."

"Follow me then. I'll give you the basics."

She showed me the lunch room and the reception area, which I already knew well. She showed me the desk where I would sit, which to my dismay, was right outside of Mr. Hardy's office. He obviously wasn't kidding when he said that I would be at his beck and call. She pointed out Ms. Swanson's desk in the right corner of the office. She then led me toward the back area of the office, where her desk and a desk for a customer service associate were situated.

"Alyssa, what do you do here?"

"He didn't explain it to you?"

"He didn't explain much."

She giggled. "That doesn't surprise me. So why did you take the job?"

Because I'm enamored with the hot guy. "The idea of travel seemed rather interesting."

"Hmm, that's funny. Because Lance always complains about it."

"Lance? Do you call him by his first name?"

"What did you think we called him?"

I fidgeted a bit. "Well, he seemed so formal in the interview."

"Don't let that fool you. He's pretty laid back. We're all about the same age here, so we have an understanding. Don't get me wrong, though. We work hard. But we also stick together, like family. You know?"

I nodded, but I didn't know. I had never felt like that at a job before. I had always felt like an outsider looking in.

"He looked pretty young. How old is Lance?"

"Thirty-three. How old are you?" Alyssa inquired.

"Thirty."

"See, I told you that we are all about the same age."

"So you never answered me. What do you do here?"

She laughed and waved her hand in front of her face. "Sorry, I got sidetracked. I'm a Certified Financial Planner. I prepare all the proposals and performance reviews for our clients. But now *you* are going to help me with that. I can give you the data, and you can develop the presentations. You know Word, Powerpoint, and Excel, right?"

"Yes. But do you have templates to work off of?"

"I do. But I think Lance wants you to improve upon them."

I bit my lip. I hoped that I would be able to do this. At my previous job I answered phones, placed trades, and did normal admin, such as opening accounts, changing addresses, and issuing checks. This position sounded completely different, and I hoped that I was truly ready for it.

Alyssa sensed my concern. "Don't worry. I'll be here. I can help you if you need me."

I smiled at her. She seemed very nice, just like Ms. Swanson. But that reminded me. I looked around to make sure we were still alone.

I whispered, "What's up with that receptionist? She didn't seem that friendly to me."

A smirk grew on Alyssa's face. "Marlene? Don't worry about her. She wanted your job. That's all."

Gasp! "Why didn't she get it?"

"Because Lance didn't want to spend that much time with her."

That made sense. "Will she ever be nice to me?"

Alyssa shrugged. "Do you care? I don't."

She was as blunt as her boss was. I wondered if she got that from him, or was that the normal air of a person who works in a hi-fi Manhattan office.

"But you said that this office is like a family."

"I did. And she's the black sheep."

I hope I never achieve that status.

Alyssa walked away, and she waved at me to follow her. "The others will be here soon. Why don't I help you get logged into the system?"

I thought about it for a second and then asked, "Can you get me a keycard and a key to the front door while you're at it."

"I'm sorry. You'll have to ask your best friend Marlene for that."

It's going to be a long day...

Alyssa showed me a few things on the computer system before I heard a familiar voice. "I knew that you'd be here."

I turned around, and it was Ms. Swanson.

I smiled and said, "I knew I'd be here too."

She laughed. "Well, I'm glad. We could use your help."

"Ms. Swanson, what do you do for the team?"

"Ms. Swanson? Pffft. You have to be kidding, right?"

"I don't know your first name."

Alyssa giggled. "I'm sorry. I guess I should have told you. It's Maria."

Maria acknowledged Alyssa and turned her head back to me. "I'm the administrator for the office."

"Which means that Maria is actually the one in charge of us all."

That brought a huge smile to Maria's face. "I don't know about that."

"And now that you're here, I'm going to put you *in charge* of our new recruit."

"I guess I should have seen it coming."

"You definitely should have."

Before Alyssa could escape to her desk, another voice rang through the office. "Hey girl, whassup?"

Alyssa cocked her head toward the sound, and then her smile spread clear across her face.

A short, tanned girl with long, dark blond hair came into view. She was quite cute and stepped with confidence. Her hair was pulled back into a pony tail that lay flat on her back and flowed down to her hips. Her clothes weren't as formal as those of the other women in the office. She was very well dressed but not in a suit. Instead, she wore a black blouse, a beige vest, and black trousers.

"What's up yourself? How was your weekend?" Alyssa asked.

"Same ol'. You know." She then noticed me. "Is this the new girl?"

She nodded as she looked me up and down. "Wow, she's pretty. What a surprise."

What's that supposed to mean? "Thanks...I think?"

"Now, Julie. Don't give out all our secrets in the first few seconds that you meet someone," Maria warned.

"What? He never hires a male, and all of his assistants are attractive. That isn't a secret."

"Don't mind her. She *loves* herself." Alyssa giggled.

"I do. I really do."

Wow. Insanity must run amok in this office. "Why does he only hire attractive women? Is there something I should know?"

Julie hmpfed before she answered, "There's a lot you should know."

Alyssa elbowed Julie. "I think you're getting the wrong idea. Lance likes women because he feels that females will take care of him, like a mother would."

Julie wasn't going to get taken out of the conversation that easily.

She interjected, "He also feels that we're a reflection of him. So he never hires ugly."

"That's good to know. Because I was planning on going ugly next week," I teased.

Julie laughed out loud. And when I say *out loud*, well, she is plain out *loud*.

"I like this girl. I hope she'll stick around," Julie said as she walked with Alyssa to their area at the back of the office.

They looked like fric and frac. They were the same height and were instantly chatting away as they disappeared out of sight. The only difference between the two was that Julie was slightly heavier than Alyssa. That wasn't a bad thing, because Alyssa was probably too thin. Julie had more curves.

A few minutes later, Marlene arrived. She got to work right on time and not a moment sooner. I guessed that she didn't want to spend any more time in this place than she absolutely had to. It was sad. I felt kinda sorry for her. She had on another very nice suit, and her medium-length brown hair was pulled back away from her face by a large brown barrette at the back of her head.

Maria was a real trooper showing me the computer system. In the course of an hour, I knew how to pull up an account, check the clients' history and balances, and how to print out statements and tax documents. All the basics.

But suddenly, Maria stood straight up and whispered, "I'll catch up with you later."

Then she scurried off to her desk.

I noticed that Marlene had a similar reaction. Everyone tried to act busy.

And then I saw him.

Mr. Hardy, *Lance*, opened the glass door. It was 9:00. According to Alyssa, he was early. They probably hadn't been expecting him yet.

Could he have come early for me? Should I be flattered? No. What am I thinking?

Today he wore a slate-gray tailored suit with a striped tie. But no matter the suit, he was still impeccably dressed.

I stood as he passed my desk. He gave me a sideways glance.

"Ms. Jade," he drawled.

"You may call me Katie. May I call you Lance?"

"No." He entered his office and closed the door behind him.

That was anticlimactic. *Oh well.* I sat back down and looked at my cherry-wood desk. It contained a side area in which I could store all of my things, which was incredibly empty right now. In front of me was a computer that I could barely use, and beside the monitor was a phone that never seemed to ring. Or at least it hadn't in the last hour. *What do I do now? Maybe I should ask Maria. She might know.*

She *didn't* know.

She showed me the plane tickets for the trip that I would be taking with Lance. But that's all she had. She sent me to Alyssa to see if she needed help with the presentations.

Alyssa and Julie were already at work. Julie jabbered away with one of the clients on the phone, talking to whomever it was like they were the best of friends. Alyssa was busy doing something on her computer.

Alyssa glanced my way and asked, "Did you need something?"

"I-I...should I be helping you get a presentation done?"

"Which one?"

"Um...the one for Friday?"

"Heck no. That's been done for weeks."

"What? Mr. Hardy told me I had to be here on Monday to get ready for Friday's trip."

"Really? Then I would ask *Lance* what he wants you to do for that. Because *I* am done getting him ready."

Julie laughed, as she tried to pretend that she was actually interested in her phone call.

"He wants me to call him Mr. Hardy."

"That is absurd. Mr. Hardy's his father. He goes by Lance." Alyssa thought about it for a second and then rolled her eyes. "He's probably trying to impress you in some way. Idiot."

I just stood there motionless. *What do I do now?*

Alyssa must have heard my thoughts, because she pointed me back in the direction of Mr. Hardy. "Go barge into his office and ask him what you're supposed to do. Does he really want to pay you to sit around at your desk doing nothing?"

I shrugged but proceeded back to my area. I wasn't going to *barge* in. Who was she kidding? I hesitated in front of his door. It was made of cherry-wood and glass, but I couldn't see in. There was a white window-covering on the inside that obstructed my view.

I knocked on the door lightly and got virtually no response.

"Busy!" Lance yelled from the other side of the glass door.

Oh well. He has to come out sometime. I'll grab him then.

So what now? How about I torture Marlene for my keys? She'll love that!

Knowing what I know now, I felt kinda bad for the girl. She seemed to not get along with anyone else in the office, and in a way, I wanted to reach out to her. I couldn't help it. I had always been one to root for the underdog. But in this case, her animosity would most likely be geared toward me.

I should probably tread very lightly around her instead of being my normal over-bearing self.

"Marlene?"

"Ms. Wilson." She corrected.

Oy. What's up with the formality? She's just like Mr. Hardy. Maybe he should have picked her for my position. They would have so much in common. But nothing to talk about...

"I'm sorry. *Ms. Wilson,* I was wondering if you have my keycard and key to the front door."

"I do." She pulled a business card-sized manila envelope out of her desk. She pushed it toward me, but her face had already turned away.

I graciously took it from her and headed back to my desk. *Wow. Someone needs to get laid in the worst possible way. I wonder what she would look like if she smiled.*

But who was I to judge? I hadn't had a boyfriend in ages, and now I had a crush on my boss. A boss, I might add, who didn't even want me to call him by his first name!

I slumped down at my desk and pulled open the top drawer. I stuck my key and keycard in the front slot and then placed my elbow on the desk and lay my head on my hand.

Internet? What other choice do I have?

"Katie!" Mr. Hardy hollered from his office.

Sure. Now he needs me. Jerk-off.

I turned the doorknob and barely got in the doorway when he yelled, "Get me Maria!"

What? He called me in here for that? Has he never heard of a phone?

But heck, I wasn't busy. So I did as he commanded.

Before I returned with Maria by my side, a tall red-head in a tight crimson business suit stormed through Mr. Hardy's open door. "Lance!"

Mr. Hardy stood and said with no inflection, "Stacy, how many times have I told you not to come in here unannounced?"

Then he walked around to the front of his desk. "Where's Marlene? Why didn't she stop you?"

"Really? You think that Marlene could stop me?" Stacy challenged.

"I was hoping," Mr. Hardy said dryly.

Stacy stood there with a dangerous expression on her face. "When were you going to tell me about this weekend?"

"Never."

She pointed at him accusingly. "You knew about the party I had planned for Saturday night!"

"And you knew I didn't want to go." His voice was quiet, and his chocolate eyes stared at her without flinching.

She was taken aback for a moment, but then she continued, "Don't be silly. Who wouldn't want to go to their own party?"

"You never listen to me, do you?"

"What?"

"My point exactly."

Her face reddened and edged on matching her suit.

"Sometimes I can hardly stand you!"

"Why do you?" Lance asked with no emotion whatsoever.

How does he maintain his composure while someone yells in his face?

His dark eyes then fixed themselves on Maria and me at the doorway. Even though his expression didn't betray how he felt, I could tell that he was embarrassed.

But...the embarrassment didn't last long.

A faint smile tugged at his lips. "Katie, I have a mega-bitch of my own. Would you like to meet her?"

That was it. Stacy huffed and stomped out of his office, barely missing a physical altercation with Maria and me while barreling through the door.

After she was out of earshot, Maria smiled at me. "Don't worry. They fight like that all the time."

"Hmm." Lance returned to his chair behind the desk.

Why couldn't I let it go? It was my first day and I should have been trying to make a good impression. *But who am I kidding? I am who I am.*

"Sir, I see that she calls you Lance."

Unfazed, he shifted his big, dark eyes toward mine. "*She* had to sleep with me first."

Chapter 3

Uncertainty

I choked. I physically choked.

But as soon as I could breathe again, I sputtered, "Sir?"

Maria rolled her eyes. "Don't tease her. I think she'd rather keep calling you Mr. Hardy."

The tiny smile appeared on his lips. "Fine. Katie, *you* can call me Lance. But don't let it get around."

"Everyone calls you Lance." Maria corrected him.

"Maria, why are you here?"

"Because you had Katie get me."

"Oh, that's right." He dug into his desk for a stack of papers. "I want to call a staff meeting for the end of the day. Now that Katie's here, we're going to shift some of the responsibilities of everyone on the team."

"Thank God."

"But none of yours will change."

"Of course." Maria took the papers from him.

Lance smiled at Maria. "You're the best. You know that?"

"I know," she said with a backwards glance.

She was out of the office in an instant.

And that left...him and me.

I cleared my throat. "Well, what should I do until the meeting?"

Lance looked confused. "Didn't Alyssa give you anything to do for our trip?"

"No, sir. She said that she's done."

"Oh. Well, that's good, I suppose. Does Maria have anything for you?"

"She didn't before. But I could double check."

"Do that." Lance turned around and faced his computer.

I wonder if he knows how rude that is.

Since I was obviously dismissed, I walked out of his office and closed the door behind me. He was a piece of work. It will take time to get used to him.

Maria entertained me for the rest of the day. Dear heart. Marlene usually sorted out the mail, but today Maria showed me how to do it. That way I could work on the mail while she got some of her stuff done. Besides that, I typed a few client letters and faxed some itineraries to conference attendees.

Maria set me up on e-mail, and she assured me that I would need it for the coordination of events.

I felt bad for her. Maria seemed really busy all day. She ate lunch at her desk. She also covered the phones when Marlene took her lunch. I really hoped that Lance was kidding when he said that none of her responsibilities were going to get shifted. It didn't seem quite fair.

Alyssa and Julie went to lunch together. They told me that there were a lot of good places to eat in the general vicinity and to check it out. They said that the café on the first floor of our building was quick and cheap, so I opted for that. I brought my lunch up to the office and sat with Maria. I didn't want her to be alone, answering the phones, while everyone else left the office.

And Lance? Well, mega-bitch came back for him, and he reluctantly went to lunch with her. He didn't look happy. But after he left, Maria told me the story. Come to find out that Stacy is an Executive Director also, but she works a couple of floors down from us. She was pretty and successful, but kinda controlling. It had been only a couple of months, but Lance had already grown tired of her short leash on him. And it didn't help matters that she was *this* close to him while he was at work. He just couldn't get away from her.

"Then why doesn't he tell her that?" I asked Maria.

"You don't know Lance yet. He hates conflict. I think that he tries to keep things as peaceful as possible," she answered.

"But why? He doesn't seem happy."

"Is anyone ever happy?"

I'm sure my expression betrayed my shock at that statement. "They can be. No one has to be miserable."

"An optimist? Good! We needed one of those around here." Maria smiled, but then turned back to her computer screen.

Before I could say anything further, the phone rang again. *Darned phone. There should be a break in the middle of the day, like in a doctor's office. Especially if everyone in the office is out anyway.*

The rest of the day went pretty much the same. Alyssa relieved Maria from babysitting me long enough to show me the templates that we would use for our presentations and performance reviews. She showed me what I would need for the trip on Friday and went over everything in detail.

Before I knew it, it was 4:00 and time for the staff meeting. There was a huge conference room between where Alyssa and Julie sat and the lunch room. Inside was a cherry-wood table that sat twenty and corresponding black leather chairs to go with it.

I was the first one there, because let's face it, what else did I really have to do? I stood at the door, wondering where I should sit.

"Are you going to just stand there, or are you going to go inside?" There he was again, directly behind me.

As a matter of fact, I had to be careful in the way that I turned to see him so that I wouldn't bump into him. *How is Lance so quiet? And he obviously has no sense of personal space. I will have to nickname him ninja because one day he will cause me a heart attack and kill me with this sneak-up approach of his.*

"Um, I didn't know where to sit."

He stared straight ahead. "Sit next to me."

He was so serious that I had to laugh. "Are you sure?"

He turned his head toward mine. "What do you mean?"

"You don't seem happy about it."

"Why would I be happy?"

I choked.

I cleared my throat. "I was just kidding, sir."

"Oh." He went to the head of the conference table and gestured for me to sit at his right.

Luckily, since the conversation wasn't flowing between Lance and me, Alyssa and Julie bounced in. They sat next to each other to Lance's left. Maria followed them and sat beside me to the right.

A minute later, Marlene walked in. I could tell that she felt awkward, but she sat down next to Maria.

I asked, "Who's covering the phones."

"Voicemail. It's after market hours. We can call back after we're done. We won't be long," Lance answered.

I nodded and then fidgeted. It was probably a stupid question.

Lance announced, "I'm sure everyone's met Katie."

That statement was met with smiles and everyone acknowledging that they had, except for Marlene, who was deathly silent.

"Well, when Katie and I are in town, we are going to use her as much as we can. So here's how it will go. Marlene," he paused, and Marlene's head shot up, "when a call comes in from a client, the first person you direct the call to is Julie. Right?"

Marlene nodded.

"If Julie is tied up, then you would direct the call to Maria, correct?"

Marlene nodded again.

"Well, I want Katie to be involved too. So if someone wants to place trades or do something basic like request a check or an address change, then I want you to send those calls to Katie instead of Maria."

Marlene nodded and looked away. Maria visibly sighed.

"Then, as you all know, Katie will be arranging the conferences, travel, and client meetings. So this should help out Maria. Katie will also be responsible for putting together proposals and such, which will help out Alyssa."

"What will she be doing for me?" Julie asked.

"Not a damn thing," Lance responded.

I was shocked at first, until I took a good look at his face. His tiny smile was there.

"I knew it! Hmpf!" Julie swiveled her chair away from the table.

"Excuse me, Lance? Will Katie be helping me with covering the phones or distributing mail?" Marlene asked.

"No, she won't. She won't be here consistently enough to make that work. But she can help Maria with lunch phone coverage and maybe cover if Maria is out."

"When is Maria ever out?" Alyssa asked.

"Just in case," Lance acknowledged. "Maria, do you have the paperwork I gave you earlier?"

After Maria handed the stack of papers to him, Lance passed a copy to everyone.

"This is the itinerary for our upcoming trip and the rest of the meetings I have scheduled for the remainder of the month. I need everyone to coordinate to make sure I'm ready. Do you have any questions?"

I cleared my throat. "Don't *I* need to get you ready? Isn't that *my* job?"

He looked at me and smiled. "Yes. Yes it is. But I also know that you aren't trained in the way we do things. So I want the rest of the group to make sure that this gets done. They know that *I'm* not going to train you. It's their job. So I'm letting everyone know what to expect."

He paused and then continued, "After this month, you're going to get these packets together and coordinate with everyone else. I'll give you the names, dates, location, and time. Then you'll do the rest."

I hope I'm up to the challenge. "Okay. Thank you, sir."

"Sir?" Julie tried to stifle a laugh.

"Julie, there's a reason why I put you in the corner of the office." Lance retorted.

But he smiled at her. Julie evidently amused him too.

Julie stood, feigning offense. "I'll return to my corner then!"

"You do that," Lance said with a monotone and a noticeable smirk on his face.

"Hmpf!" And Julie was off.

Alyssa leaned toward Lance from her seat a couple of chairs down from him. "You know she'll make you pay for that later."

"I'm sure." He didn't even flinch.

"So I assume we're done here," Maria interjected.

"Yes, Maria. We're done," Lance answered.

Maria quietly stood and walked away. Marlene followed her.

"Well, I guess I'd better calm Julie down." Alyssa stood and glared at Lance. "Thank you for riling her up for me."

"No problem." And instead of completely acknowledging her, he turned his head toward me. "Did you get what you need? You can go too."

Okay, no chit-chat. I get it. Alyssa tapped her foot at the doorway and crooked a finger at me. My inquiring mind counseled my feet to move along with hers.

Alyssa murmured, "That's how he is. He'll never change. You either love him or you hate him."

I nodded and thought about it. She walked away and headed back to her desk. When I got to mine, I sat down and went over everything in my head. But, most of all, I thought about Lance.

He's so closed off from everyone. It's hard for me to imagine that this is all there is to him. He must be hiding himself in some way. But how do I find out what he's hiding if he won't let me in?

I thought about traveling with him and shuddered. I thought about sitting next to him on the plane, for hours, with nothing to talk about. *I can't just stare at him without him noticing me when we are that close!* And then there was Stacy. I would love to ask him about that relationship. But I knew that I wouldn't get a straight answer. *Ugh, that man is so complicated!*

That man suddenly stood over me and my desk.

Damn ninja!

"Do you not have anything to do?"

"Um...I just got the instructions, and everyone else went back to their desks. I thought that we would start on the list in the morning since it's almost 5:00."

"Who leaves at 5:00?" Lance asked.

"Everyone but you." Luckily Alyssa saved me at the right moment.

She appeared behind him and handed me a stack of charts and reports neatly filed in several manila folders. "Katie, I e-mailed you the files that you'll need to work on this month's projects. We can go over them in the morning."

She glared at Lance with a cocky expression, which was funny since she was only five feet tall and he was six-foot-two. Alyssa in no way seemed intimidated by him, either by his size or the fact that he was her boss.

"Fine. Since it's her first day, I will let her leave early."

"You'll let her leave on time." Alyssa corrected him.

"Do *you* want to leave on time?" Lance asked.

"Certainly." And she turned away from him before he could say anything else.

I sat there motionless, waiting to be hit by the brunt of his foul mood.

But instead, he shifted his eyes toward mine. "Go ahead and leave, Katie. Be back tomorrow at 8:00."

"What time will you be in, *Lance*?"

"Do you have to call me that?"

"Yes, I do."

"Ugh, I never should have introduced you to the three of them."

"You didn't have a choice, sir."

"I like it when you call me sir. Anyway, you don't need me for anything you're doing before the trip. So you'll see me when you see me."

"Great."

"So get going!"

I almost jumped. I quickly signed off of my computer and grabbed my things. It wasn't that early. It ended up being 4:55 before I walked out the door. I assumed that 5 minutes ahead of time was as early as my departures would get from here on out.

Weird day. But I guess I can get used to it. I liked the girls, except for Marlene, so that was always a plus.

It took forty-five minutes via subway, but I made it home to my studio apartment in Brooklyn. Living alone sucked, and not having a boyfriend sucked even more. I passed by my full-length mirror and remembered that Julie had said that I was pretty. Was she right?

Though not as tall as Maria at five-ten, I didn't feel altogether short at five-six, and I weighed only 120 pounds. I wore my thick brunette hair long and straightened the natural curls when I went to work. I had inherited my sparkling violet eyes and my fair complexion from my glamorous maternal grandmother, or so my mother had once told me in an uncharacteristic lucid moment.

Compared to Lance, I was totally tan. He was almost as white as a ghost. But I didn't mind. It seemed to work for him. He looked like an ink drawing. His straight, silky hair and large eyes were so dark, and his skin was so light. Well, I really liked the contrast. In a way, he looked like a perfect, life-sized china doll. The only difference being that he didn't look fragile. He was tall, and I really wanted to see what he had hiding underneath that suit. He had a strong jaw line and high cheekbones. He was beautiful, yet strong and masculine at the same time. If that made any sense. But then again, a lot about him didn't make sense.

He was a complete contradiction.

And thinking of that jaw line made me want to nibble on it.

Who cared about Lance? He had a girlfriend. It was time to move on. He had a life, and here I was, stuck in neutral. My last relationship had been a real disaster. All that man had cared about was himself, and he ended up cheating on me at the end. So I didn't know why I would even want a man in my life. I could take care of myself. Sex with my ex-boyfriends had been good but not magnificent. I could probably do as good a job on my own and forget the whole idea of a boyfriend.

But yet, something about Lance still intrigued me. What was it? Was it his pompous attitude? Or was it his silent, brooding nature? Which, I might add, was completely annoying at times.

He drove me crazy, and I wasn't even at work. I couldn't get that man out of my mind!

Well, I guessed that it was time to go to the bathroom and take care of myself. The thought of Lance's strong hand grasping mine after my interview clouded my better judgment. His hand had been pretty warm and large enough to completely cover mine. I briefly fantasized about other parts of my body that his hand could caress.

I couldn't think about that. He was my boss. I refused to think about him as I pleasured myself.

Who was I kidding? That's exactly what I'd be thinking about.

Chapter 4

The Law of Attraction

Tuesday, August 21, 2012 - 7:45 a.m.

Tuesday was just like Monday. The girls, minus Marlene, actually congregated at the lunch room and talked for a while. Alyssa explained to me what a normal day was like and how everyone got along when Lance was on his business trips. She explained that the atmosphere was a lot more relaxed, and the girls did more of their own thing. But if Lance was in the office, he was always able to find work for them to do.

I went to my desk and worked on the presentation for the next meeting. This conference would be in New York, so there would be no need to arrange for travel. That was a relief. But there would be a whole slide presentation to prepare, and Lance wanted me to improve upon what Alyssa had already set up. I didn't have the slightest idea how to do that. But I stared at my screen trying to figure it out when ninja appeared behind me.

"Katie, what are you doing?" He could see what I was doing because he looked at my screen from over my shoulder.

I tried to turn my head to look at him, but if I had I would have bumped right into him. In normal circumstances I would have pushed his head out of my face.

But it was Lance, so I answered, "Working on the presentations for next week."

"Oh. That's good." He turned and walked into his office and closed the door.

Yikes. I was a total lunatic. This was the guy who got me all hot and bothered? *I don't need a boyfriend. I need a shrink!*

He was here at 9:00 again. Either Alyssa was pulling my leg, or he was trying to impress me. It was weird. But before I could really inflate my ego with that thought, Julie ran right by me and barged into Lance's office.

"Dr. Rizkalla's on the line, and he's driving me crazy." She made this announcement from right inside the door.

"What'd you do?" Lance calmly asked.

"Nothing. He's a freak. You need to talk to him!"

"Fine. Tell me what he wants first."

Julie put her hand on her hip. "He doesn't know why he has to wait three," she used her other hand to raise three fingers for effect, "business days for the funds to settle before he gets his money. I've told him and told him, but he just doesn't get it!"

Lance put his hand up in front of his face. "I'll talk to him. What line's he on?"

"My line, 1713."

Lance faced his computer screen and the phone beside it. He talked to the client in a sure, empathizing voice. Not to mention that the normal sound of his voice was all it took to soothe someone, anyway. I could tell that he was going to be able to diffuse the situation.

Julie nodded at me as she closed the door.

I turned back to my computer screen, figuring that the drama was over. *Silly me.*

In the corner of my eye appeared the large, balding man again. I remembered how he had been when I left my interview, and I couldn't help but cringe at the sight of him.

This time he was much friendlier, though. "Well, hello. You must be Katie."

I looked at him, and it felt like my eyes were bugging out of my head. "How do you know my name?"

"I'm your boss."

"Eh..." This was all I could struggle to say.

He grinned. "My name's Led Biggerstaff. I run this division. My office is on the other side of the elevator."

Lovely.

"Is Hardy available?"

Now I'm his personal secretary and his beck and call girl. Lovely, squared.

"I-I think he's on the phone with a client."

"No problem, I'll wait." And then he leaned on my desk.

Yuck. This guy was gross. It was one thing when Lance invaded my personal space. But this guy? *Ugh, I could puke right now.*

"Um, sir? May I help you with something?"

He moved a piece of paper out of the way so that he could lean in closer to me. "I don't know. What do you do?"

Oh hell. That was all-out flirting from a gross guy. I didn't know how to react. I was sure that my eyes were as huge as saucers, and my mouth was wide open. I probably couldn't say a word if I tried.

That's when ninja suddenly appeared between us. All I could see was his back.

His attention was focused on Mr. Biggerstaff. "I'm available now. Do you have something to discuss with me?"

Mr. Biggerstaff huffed. "Yeah, let's go into your office."

Boss-man led Lance into his own office. Lance didn't look happy as he shut the door.

There was no yelling, but the door remained closed for a few minutes. Then Mr. Biggerstaff left. He gave me a sideways glance as he passed me by, but that was about it.

"Katie!"

He still doesn't know how to use a phone.

I walked into Lance's office.

"Close the door."

I looked at him with a surprised expression but did as I was told.

"I'm sorry for his inappropriate behavior." He glanced at me from his desk with sadness showing through his beautiful eyes.

I returned his glance. It bothered me to see him unhappy. I didn't know what to say. He hadn't done anything wrong.

"That guy is such a lech. I try to protect you girls from him."

"Why is he like that?" I asked.

Lance shrugged. "I'm not sure. Maybe he thinks he'll get somewhere with it."

"But he's gross!"

Then my brain caught up with my mouth.

I mumbled, "I'm sorry. I know he's our boss. But he's disgusting."

Lance's tiny smile tugged at his lips. "I know he is. But he doesn't."

"That's sad."

Lance laughed. "Well, the next time he trolls around the office, completely ignore him. You don't report directly to him. And if he gets out of line, let me know."

"Thank you, sir."

"I love you, Katie."

I spun my head around so fast that I got a pain in my neck. "What was that?"

He laughed out loud. "I love it when you call me sir. You're the only one who does that."

"Oh."

"You can go back to your desk now."

"Okay, *sir*."

He smiled but then turned back to his computer screen.

After that, the drama *was* over. I didn't know whether to be happy or sad. This meant that I really needed to get to work on my presentations. I went back a few times to visit with Alyssa, and she was nice enough to give me some pointers. But the rest was up to me.

At lunch time, I offered to split phone duty with Maria. She took the first half hour, and that gave me time to grab my lunch. I took the second half hour, but she still didn't leave her desk. I could tell that she was relieved, but she only used the time to catch up on work that never seemed to cease.

Answering the phones was not that bad. For the most part, I just took messages. Most of the phone calls were for Julie, anyway. It seemed that the clients had formed a real fan club for her. It didn't surprise me. She had a bubbly personality. She was probably fun to talk to. Plus, it seemed that she took real good care of them, and who wouldn't like that?

But how did she take care of them? Julie gave their requests to Maria to process. It figured. If there was an unsung hero of the group, I would venture to say that it was Maria.

Lance had gone out to lunch. I could only assume that he met up with Stacy, but I couldn't have said for sure. He came back in a mood. He went right by my desk without even a glance in my direction.

This was ridiculous. I was going out of town with the man in a few days, and not only did I not know him, but I didn't have a clear picture of what he expected from me on this trip. *It sure would be nice to get his input on the changes I have been making on the presentations. If he doesn't like them, they'll have to be re-done. I would appreciate knowing his preferences before I devote a lot of time to the modifications.*

I hesitantly approached his closed door and lightly knocked.

"What is it Katie?"

I slowly opened the door. "How did you know it was me?"

"You're the only one who knocks that way. Heck, you're the only one who knocks." He looked at me from his desk with those big, dark-colored eyes.

I just lost my train of thought.

"Did you need something?" he asked.

"Um...yeah. About our trip this weekend."

"Are you ready?"

"Well, yes and no. Not that I have a problem, but I still don't know exactly what I should be doing."

"Whatever I ask you to do."

I cleared my throat. I knew what I'd *like* him to ask me. And it had nothing to do with charts or client data.

"Um...sir. I really want to do a good job, so I'd like to be prepared."

"You read the itinerary, right?"

"Yes sir, I did. But there are some things that an itinerary can't explain."

"Like what?"

And then...nothing came to my suddenly dysfunctional mind. The man made me nervous like crazy, and it was hard to concentrate around him. I gazed into his eyes and then, for no reason at all, my focus shifted to the painting that hung right above him in my line of sight. The picture depicting the young woman and the little boy sitting on her lap decided to haunt me. I wanted to know why she had Lance's eyes.

Suddenly, curiosity decided to kill the cat. It had been brewing since the first time I laid eyes on the image.

"Who is the woman in the painting?"

That threw him off guard. His usually stoic expression softened and was replaced with something I could only describe as sadness and doubt.

But as I saw him do with Stacy, he regrouped pretty quickly.

"Katie, did you come in here for a specific purpose?"

And now I'm embarrassed.

"Um, is it personal? I'm sorry for bringing it up." My face was red, and I started to look at everything else in the room but his eyes.

Lance huffed. "It's my mom, okay?"

That made sense.

"Oh, so you're the little boy?"

I grinned, thinking how cute he was when he was little.

"No."

Wow, that was direct. He glared at me and communicated with his expression and body language that he didn't wish to pursue this any further. Quite frankly, I would have been too scared to even peep at that moment.

I backed out of the office, and Lance said, "Was that all you needed?"

I'm a doofus and I know it.

"I'm sorry, Lance. I'm a bit apprehensive about our upcoming trip. Don't you ever get nervous?"

"No."

Okay, going nowhere fast.

I think he picked up on my feelings and did not want to make me feel worse.

He approached me from the other side of his desk. "I don't blame you for feeling nervous. It's your first time. But don't worry. I'll guide you through it."

He placed his hand on the small of my back and motioned me out the door of his office.

My feet moved, but my mind refused to follow them. "I'm glad my first time will be with you."

Holy crap! That didn't come out right. Three shades of crimson crept from my cleavage up to my artificially straightened bangs. My black pumps halted their advance of their own volition, and the horror of the situation now becoming all too clear to me.

He smiled. He must have picked up on it too.

"Don't worry Katie. But for now, I have to make some client calls. So we'll talk about this later, okay?"

I nodded, and he closed the door. I slumped over to my desk.

I should quit right now. This isn't working. I turn to mush every time that man touches me.

He touches me? Wait, that doesn't sound right. But yeah, this is the second time that he has touched me! Could he be interested too? Was I too blind to notice?

Nah, he had Stacy. And he didn't even like her. Hmm...he didn't *even like her! Oh God.* My head was spinning so fast that I could hardly breathe.

Maybe next time I should grab him. Perhaps his ass? Ack, Katie! Get a grip before you thoroughly humiliate yourself in front of your new boss.

I plopped my head into my hands. Me arguing with myself was exhausting. I lifted my head to look at my computer screen and saw the presentation. *Oh hell. I didn't even mention it.*

What should I do? Well, I could ask Alyssa. I could lie and tell her that I asked Lance, and he deferred the decision to her. That wouldn't be totally unbelievable.

I printed out the work I had done and walked to the back of the office. She chit-chatted with Julie, so I didn't feel too bad interrupting. I showed everything to her, and she mostly nodded. She pointed out a few minor errors, but for the most part, I felt good about it. Not bad for my *first time. Yikes...*

Since I obviously hadn't gotten him out of my head, I asked Alyssa, "Do you know what I should do on this trip on Friday?"

Alyssa squinted at me. "Besides what's on the itinerary?"

Yep. She was just like Lance in her answers. How did they coordinate so well?

I turned away, but then I heard Julie laugh.

Alyssa continued, "What did Lance say?"

"Absolutely nothing," I answered.

"Figures."

"So what do I do?"

Alyssa sighed. "None of us have ever accompanied him on his trips. To be honest, we don't even know why he wants someone there. He's perfectly capable on his own. So I guess just watch him and try to pick up on things. And I'm sure he will be bossing you around the whole time."

"That's for sure," Julie interjected.

I looked at the two of them, and I couldn't help it.

I had to ask, "Can you tell me a little more about Lance? You all seem so relaxed around him, but he makes me nervous. What do I do about that?"

"Relax."

Oh God. That wasn't one of the girls answering me. I looked at them, and both of their jaws had hit the floor.

I could feel it. He stood right behind me, invading my personal space again.

I slowly turned my head and looked at him with my mouth wide open. *I could just crawl under a rock and die.*

"Is that the presentation for me to look at?" He tried to take it out of my hands, but instead of handing it to him, the papers fell out of my grasp and onto the floor.

"I'm sorry, sir." I bent down to pick up the papers.

"Nice mini-skirt."

Oh crap. Most normal people would have bent down at the knees. But me? I chose to stick my ass in his face.

I peered at him, and I'm sure my cheeks were redder than Santa Claus's outfit. "This presentation isn't ready. Alyssa pointed out a couple of things to fix. May I bring it to you in a couple of minutes?"

I finished picking up the last paper and stood again.

"That's fine. I came out looking for you, and you weren't at your desk."

"Sorry, sir. I just wanted Alyssa's input."

"Understood." He took two steps.

"Sir?"

He stopped mid-stride and gave me a backwards glance.

"Why were you looking for me?"

"It was nothing. I thought I cut you off before, and I didn't want you thinking I was an asshole."

"But you are!" Julie shouted out.

"It only gets worse." He countered back at her.

Then he was gone.

I stood there frozen with disorganized papers in my arms. Some of them were upside down, and most were sticking out from one side or the other.

I had started back to my desk when I heard Julie say, "She's got it bad, don't she?"

Alyssa didn't answer. She was probably trying to spare my feelings. But I couldn't even look at them. I kept on walking until I made it back to my desk.

I made Alyssa's changes and reprinted the presentation. But Lance didn't leave his office until 5:00.

When he acknowledged me on his way out, I asked, "Do you want to see the presentation now?"

He shook his head. "Just put it on my desk. I'll review it in the morning."

"Um, okay." My hands were sweating, and I fidgeted with my fingers. "I'm sorry about earlier."

"What do you mean?"

"Talking about you to Alyssa and Julie."

"Oh, that? Don't worry. I'm sorry I make you nervous. I don't mean to." He patted my shoulder a couple of times and then walked toward the front of the office and out the door.

I knew he patted me on the shoulder in an attempt to make me *less* nervous. But how do I tell him that when he touches me, he makes me *more* nervous.

I would think that he was just a touchy-feely kind of person. But I hadn't seen him touch any of the other girls. Maybe I missed it? I didn't know. But if I had been slightly conflicted yesterday, then I was outright discombobulated today.

I need to quit. I needed to work for an ugly female. Otherwise, I would never be able to concentrate. I'd tell him in the morning. I couldn't keep going on like this.

Chapter 5

Fascination

Wednesday, August 22, 2012 - 7:45 a.m.

I was determined. Today was the day. I couldn't deal with this school-girl crush on the boss. I had to tell him that I could no longer work for him.

When I arrived at 7:45 in the morning, Lance was already there. Maria and Alyssa were there, and they looked as surprised as I did. He had bought breakfast for everyone in the office, and the three of them were setting it out in the lunch room when I arrived.

When he noticed me, he nodded. "Katie."

And he turned back around.

"What's the occasion?" I asked.

"Do I need an occasion?"

"Um, I guess not. Does this happen regularly?"

"It never happens," Alyssa answered.

"That's not true." Lance sounded hurt.

Alyssa giggled. "Fine. But it doesn't happen often. So take advantage, Katie."

I grabbed a bagel. I sliced it and put it in the toaster.

Then I looked at Lance. "I know someone's been lying to me, because you are very early this morning."

"Don't get used to it," Maria interjected.

Lance smiled. "She's right. Don't get used to it. I don't want you to be disappointed."

"Like you could disappoint her." Alyssa rolled her eyes.

I looked at her with a shocked expression. I wanted to die right there. *Okay, let me faint. That would be easier.* I counted to ten, and unfortunately, I was still conscious. I would actually have to deal with this situation, and in front of Maria and Alyssa. *Fabulous...*

Then Julie walked in. *Even better.*

"Hey girls and..." She looked confused. "Lance?"

He gave her a stern look. "Julie."

"What the hell are you doing here?"

"Why? Do you not want me here?"

"No one wants to see you in the morning. Now we have to start work immediately!"

Lance smiled even bigger. Julie *does* amuse him.

"I'll have to come in early every day then."

"No!" She ran to her desk without even getting any food.

Alyssa laughed, but then she looked at me. "Katie, your bagel's burning."

Oh, crap. Nothing says, Take me, I'm yours better than a woman who can't cook. And toasting a bagel is pretty darned simple.

I darted over and popped the thing out of the toaster. It was black and smoking. I tried to pull it out and ended up burning my fingers. I tossed it in the trash and ran to the sink to run cold water over my hand.

"That's going to stink up the whole office," Alyssa observed.

I turned my head toward hers and talked over the running water. "I'm sorry. I thought it would take longer to toast. It wasn't in there that long."

Lance walked up to me. "Don't worry about it. You'll get used to that toaster."

"What's that smell?" Julie was back.

Then she saw Lance, who was directly over me. I was still bent over the sink, and he was just behind me. She then sniffed around and noticed the black bagel in the garbage.

She looked at Alyssa and asked, "Katie burnt the bagel, right?"

Alyssa nodded.

"Lance, don't get near her. She'll end up burning down the building."

I froze immediately. That was it. *I am toast.* I slammed the water off and snaked my way out of my position between the sink and Lance.

I was in the process of slinking back to my desk when I heard Lance say, "Knock it off, Julie. You're making her feel insecure. She's nervous enough. Don't you remember when you first started?"

"I was never like that," Julie announced.

"Well, that's a shame. Because I think she's really trying. I won't forgive you if you ruin it for her."

Julie looked visibly shocked.

But it didn't take her long to recover. "Can I still get something to eat?"

"Fine." Lance motioned toward the table. "But now that you're all here, I wanted to let everyone know that I'm taking tomorrow off."

"What?" Maria asked.

He nodded. "Yep. I need to take care of a few things at home before the trip on Friday."

"You have nothing at home," Alyssa observed.

Lance huffed. "It just so happens that my mom's in town."

"Mom's here from Japan?" Julie asked excitedly. "Will you bring her in?"

"Nope."

"How 'bout her cooking?"

"Nope."

His mom! The woman from the painting. I would love to meet her. Why couldn't he bring her in?

But then my brain switched gears.

"You're Japanese?" I asked.

With a name like Lance Hardy, how does he end up being Japanese?

He shook his head. "My mom is. My dad was American, but he passed away five years ago. She moved back home afterwards."

"She makes the best Japanese food you've ever tasted," Alyssa interjected.

"And it's all for me," Lance said.

"Selfish," Julie accused.

"Hey. That's why I brought you food this morning. Now take it, and go get to work."

She stuck her tongue out at him but went ahead and did as she was told.

I went back to my desk after that. I didn't know if I was relieved that he wouldn't be in tomorrow or scared. It was the last day before our trip. What if I had last minute questions for him? Now, I would just end up meeting him at the airport beforehand.

But I have to say, I thought it was sweet that he was spending the day with his mother. I had heard that men who treat their mothers well will treat their wives the same way. Just the thought of it, well...it made me think *even more* impure thoughts about him. And there were enough of those going on already.

As he passed me on the way to his office, I said to him, "I wish I could meet your mother. It looks like everyone else has."

I smiled at him, and I'm sure I was giving him puppy dog eyes.

Ironically, he faced me with an expression that looked more like a lost little boy. "No one's meeting her this time. I have only one day with her, and I want it to be just the two of us."

I thought about it for a second. "Isn't Stacy going with you?"

He furrowed his eyebrows at the thought. "Why would Stacy come?"

And with that he walked into his office and closed the door.

Well, that's weird. Lance's mother was in town from overseas, and he had no intention of allowing Stacy to spend any time with her. This may be their only opportunity to meet for who knows how long. *Very strange. I don't understand their relationship at all. If it was me, I would want my mother to meet my boyfriend. That is...if he was important to me.*

I sat there for a second, deep in thought. I wondered how often his mother made it to the states. And she certainly wouldn't have come all that way to spend only one day with her son. Did he have siblings? What about the little boy in the picture, which Lance had clearly said wasn't him?

Perhaps his mother had been here all week and he just hadn't mentioned it? *Weird, squared.* That man was such an enigma.

He's half Japanese. I should have figured. That's where he got those dark brown eyes, which were almost black and the silky raven hair. His American father must have been an albino to make him as pale as he was. But his skin was absolutely flawless. That must be the Japanese side of the family. I certainly didn't get the same from my American lineage. And I was sure he didn't spend all night on skin care like most women did.

Hmm, he seems even more exotic now. I wondered what kind of customs he had picked up from his mother. He was quiet in nature. That must have been from her.

I really wished I could meet her. The painting of her was so stunning, and I really wanted to get to know her. The fact that her son had a painting of her in his office was kinda unusual.

Why did she have such a profound effect on him?

I shook all of those crazy thoughts out of my head. They were better saved for another time. I faced my computer and turned it on. This was my last day to prepare for the trip *with Lance.* I should probably make the most of it.

And then I remembered. My presentation was on his desk. Now, of course, he would look at it when he got a chance. Then he'd come out to tell me his thoughts.

But now I had an excuse to barge into his office. So that's what I was going to do.

By knocking. Quietly.

"What is it, Katie?"

Dammit.

I slowly turned the door knob and peered in. "S-sir, I wanted to know if you've had a chance to review my presentation."

He looked at me from behind his desk. "I just got here, Katie. You saw that."

"I know. I'm sorry, sir. I was excited to hear your thoughts."

He sighed. "Have a seat."

He motioned to the chair that I had sat in for my interview. *Yep, it was kinda weird.*

"I'm not a morning person, so you'll have to bear with me." He picked up the papers and glanced through them.

"Do you want me to get you some coffee?"

He shook his head as he read. "Never drink it."

"Why not? It might help you wake up in the morning."

His focus momentarily shifted from the presentation to look me in the eyes. "I don't like it, and I have enough stamina without it."

Stamina? Does he mean energy? Because otherwise, I know of something else that would be much better suited for his stamina...

But not with Stacy.

That wench.

"Katie, are you thinking about something?"

"Huh, what was that, sir?"

He looked at me curiously. "You seemed to be lost there for a second. Were you thinking about the trip?"

"Yes. Yes sir, I was."

"Don't be so nervous. I'll be doing most of the work. There's no way you can mess up."

Unless I ravage the boss senseless. "I know, sir. I just want to do a good job. For you, sir."

He smiled. "Can you say sir a few more times?"

That perked me up.

I saluted him and said, "Sir, yes sir, sir."

He laughed. I didn't get to hear his laugh often. It was kinda nice.

He put my presentation on his desk and marked up a couple of pages. "This was a good job, Katie. I like the visual changes you made. I just want you to make a few corrections to the data. That's all."

"Thank you, sir."

"You're welcome. Now get out of here. I have work to do." He turned toward his screen like he usually did.

But this time, he looked over his shoulder and gave me his tiny smile.

I loved it.

I walked out of his office with a smile of my own. I closed the door behind me, sighed, and strolled to my desk. What was I going to do tomorrow? No offense to the other girls, but it just wouldn't be the same without him in the office.

Chapter 6

The Chase

Friday, August 24, 2012 - 7:00 a.m.

I was at JFK. Lance wasn't with me. At least, not yet. But I was worried. Our plane was supposed to take off in an hour, and I hadn't heard from him since Wednesday at 4:00 p.m.

He had been preoccupied, and I couldn't blame him. He wanted to get home so he could spend some time with his mom. He had worked through lunch, and the whole afternoon he had been antsy. Then he left.

I spent the rest of Wednesday helping Maria out. She appreciated it. I liked helping her. She had such a kind spirit. It was nice being around her.

Thursday? Boring as hell. Alyssa was right. When Lance wasn't in the office, the girls found things to keep them occupied that weren't related to work in the least. Even Maria found some spare time to take a lunch. I covered the phones for her, because really, I had nothing else to do.

But now, I'm at the airport, itinerary and boarding pass in hand, and Lance isn't here.

Before he left on Wednesday, he suggested that I bring a swimsuit. *Why do I need a swimsuit on a business trip?*

Lance had read my thoughts. "We're staying at a nice hotel. We may have time for a swim. My swimsuit is already packed."

So of course I brought mine. Like I was going to miss out on *that* opportunity.

Who was I kidding? Wednesday night I bought a new swimsuit! I had dashed to Bloomingdale's after work to scour the racks for a new swimsuit that I hoped would be incendiary enough to inspire Lance into the kind of action that I had been dreaming of since I met him. While I was looking, the smallest bikini in the whole store jumped off the rounder of clearance items right into my hands. The skimpy magenta-paisley-on-aubergine-background suit barely covered all the necessary areas and brought out the violet in my eyes perfectly. Swimming in it might be dicey, however. *Oh, well. I can sit out in the sun and watch him swim, if it comes to that.*

Actually, I hoped it would come to that. The thought of Lance half naked and completely wet made me tingle.

Just at the moment that the tingle made its way to my vagina, Lance suddenly stood in front of me. *Holy crap! If he doesn't stop doing that, one of these days I'm going to pass out from the shock.*

"What's wrong, Katie?" I caught the perplexed tone in Lance's voice.

With me sitting in this uncomfortable plastic airport chair and Lance standing there before me, he truly did tower over me. He wore a white dress shirt, bright yellow tie, and navy blue suit pants.

"Nothing sir."

"You were worried that I wouldn't show up, weren't you?"

Yep, that was it. I was glad that reading my mind wasn't one of his fortes.

"No sir. I knew I was early."

"Oh, that's good." He sat beside me and leaned toward my seat. "So, are you excited?"

I was. But it had nothing to do with the trip and everything to do with him leaning over my chair. "Yes I am, sir."

"Do you call me sir when you're nervous?"

"No, I call you sir because you said you like it."

"Oh. Well, that's good." He leaned back into his own chair.

"How was your day off?" I looked at him expectantly.

He stared off into the distance. "It was interesting."

As descriptive as ever. He has a real talent for vague.

"What did you do?" I asked.

"Not much."

I groaned loud enough that he could hear it.

"Does your mom like to visit her friends in New York while she's here?"

He looked confused. "What friends?"

"Aren't you from New York?"

"Oh, no. My dad was a Brigadier General. His last post was at Headquarters Marine Corps in DC. Then he retired there."

I can see that strict military demeanor in Lance. That makes a lot of sense.

"Really? So how did your parents meet?"

"Is this twenty questions?" he asked.

"Just trying to pass the time, sir."

He waved his hand in front of his face. "You don't have to entertain me, Katie. That's not part of your job."

But I'd like to entertain you. In ways you can't even imagine.

"I'm sorry." I turned my head away from him.

He leaned over my chair again, in an attempt to look me in the face, even though I had turned away. "Aw, Katie. I didn't mean it like that."

He took a deep breath and exhaled. "Fine. My dad's first post was in Japan. He met my mom and thought she was pretty cute."

According to her picture, she was downright beautiful. And her beauty wasn't lost on her son.

"She said that he was good looking too, and he was very kind. A lot kinder than any other man she had ever met."

And that's where Lance gets his personality.

"He courted her for a year before proposing to her. She loved him, but the transition of moving to the states was more than she bargained for. She missed her family. That's why she went back after he was gone."

I crinkled my eyebrows as I thought about that. "What about you?"

"What about me?"

"Didn't she want to stay here to be near you?"

"Oh, Katie. I had already left for New York. And I'm never home. She can't live her life around my schedule. Besides, after my dad died, she said there were too many painful memories for her to stay here."

Painful memories? That's sad. "So how long is she here for?"

"She's leaving today."

Curious. "How long was her stay?"

"A week."

"Why didn't you take more time off?"

"I did. I don't normally leave at 5:00 every day. What did you think I was doing?"

"I didn't know, sir."

He smiled. "I suppose you didn't."

"Do you have any brothers or sisters?"

"No." He seethed.

Wow. Is that a sore subject? But I never know when to quit.

"Who is the little boy in the picture?"

He didn't answer. He just shifted his focus from me to the gate. *Like an empty gate is over-the-top interesting...*

I timidly placed my hand over his. "Lance, the picture is in your office. Why is it such a big secret?"

His eyebrows furrowed as he studied my hand on his. Then he slowly rotated his wrist so that he could intertwine his fingers with mine and give me a slight squeeze.

"It was my brother."

What? "But you just said..."

"How about you?" he asked.

I knew that he was intentionally distracting me by changing the subject. But it worked, mainly because he still held my hand.

"What about me?"

"Do you have brothers or sisters?"

I looked at our hands, which were still positioned on his lap. "No."

"Why not?"

"I was raised by a single mom."

Then the attendant announced our flight. I peered in the direction of our gate. People were already lining up. I reluctantly let go of his hand and headed toward the end of the line.

Thank God. I didn't want to tell him that I didn't even know who my father was. That was a real downer, and I really didn't want to go into it. But it was my own fault. I had brought up the subject.

By comparison, he grew up in a fairy tale. It figured. I had always wanted the fairy tale that most people took for granted.

But then again, what's up with his brother? He said he didn't have any siblings and then used the past tense to describe him. What happened? It was painful enough to get him to confide in me this far. Would I ever get the truth out of him?

When we found our seats on the plane, Lance took the window, and I sat next to him in the middle seat. A minute later, a rather large man sat next to me on the aisle. He took up a seat and a half, and therefore was pressed up against me.

Personal space. I like it. Only Lance seemed to be able to invade my personal space without me getting irked. And that's only because I have a huge crush on him. This was a six hour flight to San Diego, and I was *really* not looking forward to spending that time constantly touching the stranger beside me.

I scooted closer to Lance.

Like that was a bad thing.

He looked at me curiously. There I was, all over the arm rest and leaning toward him. I owed him an explanation but couldn't say a word. So facing him directly, I motioned with my eyes toward the man in the other seat.

"Oh," he said.

I leaned over Lance to look out the window. "May I have the window seat this time?"

Like we do this all the time...but the guy to my left didn't know that.

"Not a chance," Lance replied dryly.

Rat bastard.

I looked him directly in the eyes and tried to communicate through my expression. *You know I'll be getting you back for this later, right?*

In response, he gave me his tiny little smile and turned his head to look out the window again.

So...I am going to stay pressed up against Lance for six hours. Things could definitely be worse.

But the thing was, if anyone saw us, we looked more like boyfriend and girlfriend than boss and employee. The impromptu hand holding in the airport lobby didn't help.

Maybe I'm the only one who's confused. No one on the plane cared about our relationship, except for me. Our close proximity was doing terrible things to all of my senses.

I could smell his cologne again. I didn't recognize the scent. And I couldn't ask him. That would be weird. It wasn't overpowering, but it was alluring. It made me pay attention to his neck, which innocently peeked out above his white dress shirt. I briefly thought about kissing his neck, all the way up to that jaw line of his. *Yikes!* I must have a jaw line fetish because the thought of nibbling on his jaw got me hot. And I was too close to him to be getting this excited!

I tried to turn away but couldn't. He had such a beautiful profile. I knew it was weird to think of a man as beautiful, but he was. I couldn't help but stare. He had a small, perfect nose...and that jaw line. *Eek!* There it was again. And those dark eyes and silky black hair. His hair looked nicer than most women's hair did. I wanted to run my fingers through it. Right then. While nibbling along his jaw...

"Katie."

That shook me out of my thoughts. "Uh, yes, Lance?"

"You can stop crushing my hand now."

I looked down, and *oh God*, when did I start clutching his hand so tightly? When did I touch his hand at all? I pulled my hand back instantly. And, of course, noticed that it was sweating.

Get me off this plane.

"I-I'm afraid of flying," I said with as much innocence as I could muster.

He furrowed his eyebrows. "Seriously? Why didn't you tell me before?"

"I-I thought you wouldn't hire me."

"Oh, I'm sorry. I wish I had known. I'm sure there's something you could take to calm your nerves." He looked around. "I'll order you a drink when we're up in the air."

He then looked back out the window.

That's all I needed. What kind of fool would I become after I added some alcohol to my system? Besides, I hardly ever drank.

But how could I tell him the truth? It was better to stick to the lie at this point.

The flight attendant announced that we would be taking off, and he went through the required safety demonstration. Then we were off.

The long flight didn't seem so long. There was a movie, and of course the rum and Coke that Lance ordered did calm my nerves. And then I woke up...

What the hell?

I woke up when I felt Lance stroke my hair and whisper in my ear, "Katie, we're here."

I slowly lifted my head off of his shoulder. *Oh God, I hope I didn't drool.* I looked at his white dress shirt in panic. *Phew.* No signs of drool or wayward make-up. I must have been lying with my hair between his shoulder and the side of my face to spare his shirt like that. *Thank God. I'm saved.*

"I fell asleep?"

"Don't worry about it. It was probably the rum. But the good news is that you weren't scared about flying, right?"

Yeah. But now I'm scared about sexually harassing the boss.

"I-I'm sorry. That must've been awkward for you."

He waved his hand. "Don't worry about it. We're here. So let's hurry and get our things once the door opens. We need to drop off our bags at the hotel and then head over to the convention center."

He looked at me. "It's a good thing you're well rested, because it's going to be a long day."

Great. Well, you should be well rested too, because I want to ravage you later. Whoops. Did I just think that? Why yes! Yes I did!

We got to the hotel, and boy, was it nice. I asked Lance how expensive it was, and he assured me that the company probably got deep discounts from the hotel chain due to its constant travel requirements.

The rooms? Nicer than my apartment. But what really caught my eye was that we had adjoining rooms.

Wait. Wait for it...adjoining rooms? My head exploded, along with the rest of me!

What in the hell was this man trying to do to me? However, I gave him the benefit of the doubt. Maybe he just asked for our rooms to be side-by-side and someone at the hotel gave us adjoining rooms. But either way, this temptation was getting to be too great for me to handle.

I dropped my bag on the bed, and yeah, I couldn't wait to make it obvious that the only thing that separated me from my very hot boss was a door that was easily opened...for you know...easy access.

I opened the door in my room and knocked on the door of his room... quietly.

Dammit. Why am I always so formal with this guy?

A few seconds later, he opened his door and asked, "You're done already?"

"Done with what?"

He furrowed his eyebrows. "Don't you want to freshen up before we head out?"

With a scared expression, I asked, "Do I need to?"

He gave me that tiny smile. "You may want to fix your hair. I think you ruffled it up while you slept."

My right hand shot up quickly to pat down my hair. "Oh my God! Why didn't you tell me before?"

He laughed. "I didn't want to embarrass you. Until now."

That's great.

"I'll meet you outside that door," he pointed to the front door of his room, "in a few minutes."

He gave me a sly look as his face disappeared behind the closing door.

He's a little imp. Who would've guessed? I wonder what other embarrassing things he was going to just let me do in public. Well wait, whatever it is, I might like it. And it may involve my hair getting messed up. But then again, what's a little messed up hair between friends?

After I was done brushing my hair and re-applying some make-up, I met him outside of our rooms. He now wore the navy blue jacket to match his pants. He looked stunning. He was very professional looking. This was the nicest suit that he had worn so far.

The convention center was right across the street. We passed through security and made it to the exhibit hall directly in front of us. It was quite large. When I went in, there were long tables set up along each side of the room. There were also rows of tables facing the podium. Lance explained to me that on the right side of the room the annuity wholesalers would be set up. The money managers would be stationed on the left side.

Tonight's topic was: *The new tax laws and how they affect the high net-worth client.* There would be two speakers each from the annuity side and the money manager side. Around forty financial advisors would be in attendance.

Since Lance was the coordinator, he would do the opening and closing speeches. He would also introduce each of the speakers.

He showed me two big boxes on the podium. They were filled with packets of information for each of the FAs. Lance told me to put one at each seat, along with a pad and a pen.

As I passed everything out, the different wholesalers came in. Each one shook Lance's hand and struck up a conversation with him. It seemed that everyone knew him and knew him well.

Most of the wholesalers were men, but a few of them were women. And flirting with Lance was par for the course. It made me sick. Not only were these women impeccably dressed, but they all appeared to be surgically enhanced to look as perfect as could be. *Well, how can I possibly compete with that?*

When I was done with the packets, I asked Lance what I should do next. He told me to help all the wholesalers set up. He then asked me what I wanted to eat, since we'd be working through lunch. It was already past 12:00, which was 3:00 p.m. New York time.

"What are you having?" I asked.

"I don't eat before these things. I might get sick."

Wow, he does get nervous. I never would have guessed.

And he lied about it too!

"Then I'll manage."

"You can't do that. You're going to get hungry."

I smiled. "I'll manage."

He didn't seem happy with that answer. "Fine. But I'll order room service afterwards. My treat. Okay?"

"That sounds good." Actually that sounded better.

That sounded like I would be eating with him alone, and I'd like that a whole lot. Now, he probably meant me in my room and he in his. But I can fantasize, right?

The day went by rather quickly. The conference started at 5:00 and ended at 8:00. For most of the session, Lance and I sat at the side of the podium. I occasionally ran and got things that were needed by a speaker at the last minute. But my part certainly wasn't very taxing.

Lance? If he *was* nervous, he didn't show it. I watched him on that stage addressing the crowd. I was so proud of him. He seemed so sure of himself, and his voice was soft and smooth, yet loud enough to hear.

And he knew his stuff. *Wow, this man is intelligent too. It's almost unfair that God gave one man so many gifts.* Usually when a woman was drop-dead gorgeous, people thought that she was a ditz. But Lance had it all.

I wanted him.

Lance and I stayed until everyone left. It was 9:00 by the time all the dilly-dalliers finally decided to walk out the door. I was hungry and tired. I tried to clean up after everyone for the hour that people just stood around talking. But at 9:00, Lance told me to stop. The convention center employees would get the rest.

It was 12:00 midnight New York time. And both of us were feeling it as we walked back across the street to the hotel.

We passed the bar in the lobby, and Lance asked, "Do you want to eat here or in the room?"

I shook my head. "I'm tired. Maybe we should eat in our rooms."

"Oh." Lance hung his head.

"Do you want to eat down here?" I asked, as I stopped in the middle of the hallway.

"No. But I was hoping that we could eat together. I wanted to go over our plans for tomorrow."

Eep. This was almost too good to be true. I walked again toward the elevator.

"Do you want me to come over to your room after I get changed?" I certainly wasn't going to relax, sitting in a business suit.

"Yeah. That sounds good. Tell me what you want, and I'll order. That way the food might come by the time you arrive." We entered the elevator, and Lance pushed the button for our floor.

"What are you having?"

"Katie. I hate that. Just tell me what you like."

I gave him a perturbed look. "Nothing."

"Don't be that way. I know you have a mind of your own, and I want to know what you like to eat."

"Lance, I feel uncomfortable because you're paying. So I don't want to come off like a pig." The elevator chimed, and the door opened.

He shook his head. "I'm expensing it, so order what you want."

"Fine. Steak and lobster," I said, as we both walked out of the elevator and headed toward our rooms.

He smiled. "Or anything else that happens to be more expensive?"

"Exactly." I laughed.

We both stood in front of our rooms, messing with the keys, and Lance said, "See you in a little while."

I waved and entered my room.

Now seriously, what happens if something happens tonight? Am I really prepared for this? I wasn't sure. But I decided to *make* sure. I took a shower, shaved up, down, and sideways, and made sure that I smelled good. Well, I probably reeked when I was done from all the perfume and lotions I wore. I hoped he could choke down his food through the fumes.

I put on a loose, low cut teal top and black palazzo pants. I wanted to look nice, but I didn't want to be too obvious, just in case he had no sense of smell and couldn't detect the over-done perfume. When I did my make-up and hair, I tried to do it in a way that said *casual*, instead of *Take me, I'm yours.* But maybe I should have reconsidered that?

I knocked on his door between our two rooms, and a few seconds later, I heard the lock pop open. The door swung away from me, and Lance stood there. He had on gray sweatpants and a snug-fitting white t-shirt. His muscular biceps peeked out from under the short sleeves.

I looked at him as I walked in. I couldn't contain the grin on my face. I really hoped that I wouldn't giggle like a school girl during dinner.

Then I noticed the small, round table full of food and realized that the man wasn't kidding. Lance motioned me to my seat. The table *did* have steak and lobster on it. *Crap.* The hotel had a seafood restaurant downstairs. He must have paid extra to get something delivered from its menu.

But beside it, *oh my God*, was crème brulee.

I faced him. "How did you know?"

"What?"

"How did you know that crème brulee is my favorite dessert?"

He shrugged. "I didn't. I thought I'd give it a shot."

"I love you." But then my hands shot up to my mouth.

Why didn't I catch that before it slipped out?

Lance laughed. "Just like I love you when you call me sir?"

He saved me. I loved him even more.

"Yep. So if you give me crème brulee and I call you sir, I think we'll get along."

He reached for my hand. "Deal."

I shook his hand...and probably held onto it for a second longer than necessary. It was a nice, big, strong... *Oh, never mind.* I wasn't going to think about what he could do with hands like that.

We sat down and ate. If anything could take my mind off of Lance, then it would be this meal. It was fantastic.

I couldn't remember the last time I had eaten out. I couldn't really afford meals like this on my salary. And none of my ex-bum boyfriends could either. Not that they would spend money on me even if they did have it. So this dinner was a real treat.

As I ate my crème brulee, Lance explained the plans for tomorrow. At 10:00 a.m., we were meeting with a prospect. He had a portfolio worth $150 million, and Lance was hoping to close that deal tomorrow. After that it was a free day. We were staying overnight and would be flying back on Sunday at 11:00 a.m.

Now, call me stupid. Because I am. But I put two and two together, and it didn't equal four.

So I had to ask, "Lance. I'm sorry. But that makes me curious. Why aren't you going home early to attend Stacy's party? It seemed important to her."

He looked at his bare feet for a second. And then he placed his hands flat on the table and pushed himself up from his chair. He picked up his plate and put it on the tray that sat on a nearby shelf.

Oh God. Now I offended him. Why did I have to ask that?

He said, in a volume a little louder than a whisper, "I told her I didn't want a party."

I looked at him with a curious expression. "Party for what?"

"My birthday." He headed toward his bedroom. "I'm tired. Finish up. I'll meet you outside the front door of our rooms at 9:00."

Then he closed the bedroom door behind him.

Wow. I blew it.

They say that curiosity killed the cat. Well, it doesn't do much good for humans, either.

But wait a minute. His birthday? When is his birthday? Is it tomorrow? He certainly doesn't seem to be in a festive mood. And he didn't want to spend his birthday with his girlfriend.

Would he rather spend it here...with me?

I looked around his room. It was nice. His was a suite with a separate bedroom, and mine was a room with two double beds. Talk about the difference between boss and employee.

I couldn't really fault the guy. This trip had been fun, and I certainly couldn't afford to travel like this on my own. So who was I to complain?

I scraped up every last bit of my crème brulee and then wandered into my room.

I flopped down on my bed. *Lance is right. I'm exhausted!* But still, I was hoping that tonight would lead to more. I was disappointed. Then again, the guy did have a girlfriend. What did I really expect?

⋙✦⋘

Saturday, August 25, 2012 - 9:00 a.m.

I opened the door of my hotel room to find Lance already standing there.

"Did you eat already?" he asked.

"Did you?"

"Why do you keep doing that?"

"Doing what?"

"Don't worry about me. I asked you a question."

"My question was just as valid as yours."

He groaned. "Should we pick you up something along the way?"

"If you're hungry."

His usually peaceful face betrayed his frustration. "You're impossible."

"I know it. So let's get going." I started down the hallway toward the elevator.

Lance spoke to the valet about a taxi. The prospect's house was approximately thirty minutes away.

During the ride, we didn't say much to one another. I wanted to break the ice, but I didn't know how. He was a hard man to chit-chat with. And I certainly didn't want to bring up any sore subjects.

I cleared my throat. "Thank you again for dinner last night."

He didn't even move.

He looked out the window. "No problem."

"Are you going to speak to me?"

That made him turn toward me. "I *am* speaking to you. I just said 'no problem'."

Men. They were so different than women. It surprised me that we came from the same planet.

"You've been a little off since last night."

"Oh. Don't worry about that."

"Okay..."

Lance ran his hand through his glossy ebony locks. "Katie, this meeting is a big deal. I'm trying to focus."

That made sense. And here I was being selfish. Evidently, it *isn't* all about me.

"I'm sorry. I've never come along for a client meeting before. I didn't know."

He gave me that tiny smile of his. "That's okay."

"Is there anything I can do?"

"Oh, you will."

I didn't know if I liked the sound of that.

"Okay." I then looked out the window myself.

It wasn't that interesting, but it seemed like the only thing to do for the time being.

We arrived at the prospect's house, and I was taken aback. It was *not* a mansion. It was a modest, ordinary house.

I turned to Lance. "Are you sure this is it? Do we have the right address?"

He nodded. "Katie, this is *how* people get rich. They don't spend their money. They save every dime."

Wow. Who knew?

We walked up to the little white house and Lance knocked on the door. He stood even straighter than usual, and he clutched onto his briefcase tighter than he needed to.

Am I supposed to be nervous? Because I'm not.

A little old man, who appeared to be in his nineties, answered the door. He acknowledged Lance but then looked at me.

Through his glasses, his eyes widened. "Who is this?"

"This is Katie Jade, Dr. Floyd," Lance answered.

He looked me up and down. "She's pretty."

Then he turned around and walked toward his living room. Lance motioned me to follow him through the door. Once inside, Lance continued to follow the doctor, and I stopped to close the door behind us.

The living room had two couches sitting perpendicular to one another. Dr. Floyd sat on one, and Lance sat on the other. Lance was actually turned slightly so that he could face the doctor. I intended to sit next to Lance, but Dr. Floyd patted the seat next to him.

I looked Lance in the eyes. I tried to communicate telepathically. *What? Are you kidding?*

I could see amusement in his eyes, but his lips didn't move this time. So I sat down next to the doctor.

Yep. Now I see what Lance *really* needed me for on this trip. *That sly dog.* If he thinks he won't hear about this later, he is sadly mistaken.

Lance opened his briefcase and handed Dr. Floyd the reports that we had prepared. Then he went over the information in great detail. Plus, what impressed me most was that he was able to break everything down so that it was easy to understand without being condescending. He didn't use industry lingo. He used examples from everyday life.

It was magical. If he was nervous, no one would have guessed it. He was in his element, and it looked like he had been born to do this job. Facing him actually suited me better, as I was able to see his facial expressions. I could watch all of his different gestures as he spoke. And I was entranced.

This was his stage, and he was the master of it. If I had a whole bunch of money, I would certainly hire him to manage it. He was intelligent, approachable, and caring. And it showed.

The doctor coughed mid-way through Lance's presentation. I went to his kitchen to get him a glass of water.

As I sat back down, the doctor smiled. "I hope you'll be answering the phone when I call."

I was struck speechless.

But Lance answered for me, "Don't worry, Dr. Floyd. I'll give you Katie's cell number so that you can reach her twenty-four hours a day."

I shot Lance a look, and this time he openly smiled. He obviously loved my torment.

The rest of the meeting went well. Dr. Floyd signed the paperwork, and we were on our way. But not before he gave me a hug. It wasn't creepy. He was a sweet old man. He was probably very lonely living in that house all by himself.

Lance was a lot more relaxed on the way back. We talked about the meeting a bit, and he apologized for throwing me under the bus. But, of course, I gave him hell anyway.

When the cab pulled up to the hotel, Lance got out first.

But before he darted away, he said, "Grab your bathing suit. I'll meet you at the pool."

That was strange. "Seriously? Right now?"

"Mmhmm." And then he was off.

Okay. I was going to see him in his swimsuit. I was game. I hoped that he was ready for mine.

Chapter 7

‿⁀

Wet

Saturday, August 25, 2012 - 12:00 p.m.

The preparation that I had done last night came in handy when I had to put on my skimpy magenta-colored bikini. I freshened up before I headed downstairs to the pool. Over my swimsuit I wore a light blue-green tunic and matching sandals. The tunic fell just past my butt, so I felt weird walking around the hotel in it. But a hotel with a pool should be used to this sort of thing by now.

I entered the pool area, and Lance was nowhere in sight. But I did see a couple of full-length lounge chairs sitting next to each other. I grabbed a couple of towels from the guest station and claimed the chairs as quickly as I could. We would be right in front of the pool, so my plan to watch him swim could be realized.

As soon as I sat down, the ninja came up behind me. I must have been getting better at sensing him.

"Katie."

I looked at him. Now I could see what he was hiding under those shirts. The man was nothing but abs. He wore indigo trunks and nothing else.

Holy six pack! He didn't look like a bodybuilder. He was still thin in frame. But what he had, well, it was very nicely put together.

"Oh God," I said out loud.

I knew that I stared, but I couldn't help it. With abs like that, why did he *ever* wear a shirt? Just looking at him took my breath away.

"What's wrong?"

That snapped me out of my sexual fantasy. "Nothing."

I still couldn't take my eyes off of him.

Then there was that skin color. He was so light that he almost reflected the sun. But then again, being able to reflect the sun was kinda hot. There weren't that many people out there who could do that.

He had no tan lines. Not a surprise. I wondered how much sunscreen that man had to wear to remain that light skinned.

I patted the seat beside me. "Why don't you get some sun? You're looking a little pale today."

"I look pale every day," he deadpanned.

"Why is that?"

"My father was a red-head. I inherited his skin tone."

"How fortunate."

He squinted his eyes at me. "Does my *tan* bother you?"

I shook my head. "Not at all. Especially when you throw in those abs."

He looked toward the pool. "Oh, I get it. So my abs can stay, but my skin color's got to go?"

"Something like that." I faced the pool myself and tried not to laugh.

"Good to know. Let's go in."

And then I panicked. "Um, I can't swim."

"Yes, you can." He seized my hand and pulled me up.

Then he looked at me and furrowed his eyebrows. "Are you going to swim in that shirt?"

"I'm not going to swim. Problem solved." I tried to wriggle my hand away from his.

But I was quite unsuccessful in doing it.

"Come on, Katie. I never get to go to the pool anymore. I loved swimming as a kid." He gave me the puppy dog eyes.

"Then you go swim. I'll watch." *That was my plan anyway.*

"It's more fun if you come." Still with those puppy dog eyes.

How could I say no? "Fine."

I slowly lifted the tunic over my head. Then I saw his eyes widen.

I almost laughed. I had been waiting for this exact moment. But the man simply couldn't give me the satisfaction.

"I'll make sure that *that thing* you call a swimsuit stays on," he said with his usual monotone voice.

Or...you could simply pull it off of me in private. I wouldn't mind. But then, I get to do the same to you.

I took a good look at him as he pulled me toward the pool. Besides his naked chest, I liked his arms and legs too. I had seen his biceps yesterday, and they still didn't disappoint. And his muscular thighs and lower legs weren't hard to look at, either. I wondered how often he had to work out to maintain that body of his.

He was like a big kid in the pool. He dunked me a few times, and he loved swimming underneath the water. His movements seemed effortless. He could swim like a fish.

He laughed. I had never heard him laugh like that. It was natural and unrestrained. I could tell that he let down the façade that he usually hid behind. It was really nice to see him this way.

I didn't *swim.* I just stood in the water and watched him. My plan wasn't totally ruined. It was just a change in location. My hair was wet, thanks to Lance. But he didn't seem to mind. His black, silky hair looked just as nice slicked down as it normally did.

And seeing his half-naked body moving around in the water *did* feed into my sexual fantasy. *So good on him!*

After an hour, we got out of the pool. I followed him to the lounge chairs, and he picked up the towel that I had gotten for him earlier and dried his hair.

He faced me. "Katie, I was thinking about ordering some food. Do you want anything?"

I did. I was starved at that point. *The man never eats!*

"Sure."

"I'm going to order since you always ask what I'm having."

"Fine."

"Should I order you a drink? The poolside bar has good mixed drinks. But I don't want you falling asleep afterwards."

"Very funny."

He flashed me his tiny smile and called to a waiter. Lance ordered us both burgers and fries this time. Then he ordered a tropical fruit drink for me and a shot of sake for him.

I gave him a disgusted look. "Eww, how can you drink that stuff?"

He shrugged. "I don't know. I tried it once when I visited my mom in Japan. Since then, I guess it just relaxes me."

"It doesn't taste good."

"It's quick and easy and gets the job done. So who cares?"

It's a motto. If he ever says that he cares about something, then I'm going to keel over.

"Lance. I have to admit something to you."

"What's that?"

"I don't really drink."

He thought about that for a second. "Then why do you let me keep ordering you drinks?"

"Because you want to."

"Oh."

We ate lunch and talked. I nursed my mixed drink, and he drank a few more shots of sake. As the alcohol took over, the remaining formality between us decreased.

Lance looked at me. "You know, you should really put your shirt back on. Your breasts are going to pop out of that bathing suit."

I stood and grabbed my shirt. "Would that be a bad thing?"

"Not if you're a professional flasher."

"That's not fair. There you are exposing your whole chest and not worrying about it at all."

I put on my tunic and sat back down on the lounge chair.

"I'm a man."

"And men are pigs."

"Hey, I told you to cover up. Why does that make me a pig?"

"Because you were obviously looking."

"If you didn't want me to look, then you wouldn't have worn such a small bathing suit."

"Is that so?"

"That's so."

I huffed. He was right. So I turned away from him and blushed.

I didn't see it, but I felt it.

He placed his hand on my hand. "Don't be that way."

I faced him. "Be what way?"

"Don't be mad."

"Do I amuse you?"

With his tiny smile, he answered, "Yes, you do."

I was about to get up, but then he grasped the hand that he was touching to keep me in place. "But in a good way."

I noticed his eyes. He had such beautiful eyes. How could I turn away from such beauty?

A waiter passed by, and Lance ordered a couple of more shots of sake.

Wow, he is really throwing them back. Either he has a huge tolerance for alcohol, or he is trying to get sloshed.

And then my brain caught up.

"Lance?"

"Yes, Katie."

"Is today your birthday?"

He hesitated for a second and then nodded.

"And this is the way you wanted to spend it?"

He nodded again. "This is the best birthday that I've had since I was a kid."

"Then why are you trying to get drunk?"

That did it. Curiosity went and killed the cat again. Our hands had remained intertwined until this point, but then he pulled away.

He ran his hand through his silky locks. "Katie, there are things that I'd rather forget."

And then...he just stopped talking. I looked around, wondering if he expected *me* to fill in the blanks.

But I wasn't going to let it go that easily.

"What kind of things?"

He exhaled deeply. "I'm sorry. I can't do this."

He stood, and I knew he was pulling away from me again. It was a Lance move that I was already used to. But for some reason, I wasn't going to let him get away this time.

I rose out of my chair so that I could face him directly. I was desperate and willing to try anything to keep him from leaving.

"Lance, what do you think about me?"

"Huh?"

I leaned in closer and looked him in the eyes, "You heard me. What do you think about me?"

He looked stunned. "In what context?"

"As a woman? As a friend? I don't know. I'm just trying to figure you out."

The stunned expression remained on his face. "Oh. Well, I think you're nice and fun to be around."

Like a three hundred-pound male best friend?

I decided to just go for it.

I had to spell it out for him. I knew that if I was ever going to get a straight answer from him, it would be in an impaired state.

I should've let him have those last two shots without opening my big mouth!

So I leaned in even closer and continued to look him straight in the eyes, "Do you find me attractive?"

His eyes stared right through me, as if I wasn't even there. "It doesn't matter. You're my employee."

"I can find another job."

Then I closed the remaining distance between us. I threw my arms around his neck and pressed my lips against his. I was going for broke. But I needed to know once and for all.

At first, he didn't kiss me back. But after a few seconds, we both melted into the kiss. I ran my fingers through his hair, holding his head close to mine. He wrapped his arms around me, his right hand on my neck and his left hand at the small of my back.

His lips parted, and I could feel the tip of his tongue trace along my lips. I opened my mouth so that our tongues met. We explored each other's mouths, and I could hardly stand it anymore. I had no recollection of where we were at the moment.

And then he suddenly pulled away. He breathed heavily, but he had a sad expression on his face.

"I'm sorry," he said.

He walked away. He didn't even pick up his shoes before he left.

He was so unpredictable. *He passionately kisses me one second and then just walks away the next?*

I stood there, all by myself, and groaned out loud. *Lance felt something. I know he did. There was a definite spark between us. Why is he denying it?*

It couldn't be Stacy. Their relationship was nothing but weird. He had ditched her on his birthday.

And what is all this cryptic talk about his birthday anyway? What is he trying to forget? And why is an hour long swim in the pool the best birthday he's had since he was a kid?

The boss excuse was just plain lame. I told him I could find another job. I could turn in my resignation if that would free him up.

Ugh, that man is so confusing. I don't know if I am in love or absolutely crazy for even wanting to pursue this!

I stood and got my things and picked up his shoes as well. Then I went upstairs.

I walked to Lance's door and gently knocked. I wanted to know if he was okay.

He's a grown man, not a lost little boy! Get a grip already.

No response. I didn't know if he had decided to go somewhere or if he was ignoring me. Either way, it was obvious that I was no longer included in his plans.

I decided to take a nap. The alcohol was getting to me. I didn't drink much, but since I wasn't used to it, the buzz was taking effect. Before I fell asleep, I reviewed everything that had happened in my mind.

He had kissed me back. He *was* interested. But something was keeping him from acting on his impulses. I had to know what that was.

And that kiss? *Wow!* How could I possibly think of it and just be friends with the guy? I wanted to kiss him again...and soon! *But how do I do that if he keeps running away from me?*

I fell asleep, but as I dreamt, nothing but different scenarios ran through my mind. And they were all naughty. Even asleep, I just couldn't get that man out of my mind.

⚜

Saturday, August 25, 2012 - 7:30 p.m.

I woke up and made my decision. Someone had to make the first move.

I wanted him to pound me senseless. And I was tired of waiting. *To hell with his hot and cold games already!*

I dressed in a black silk nighty that barely covered my butt. *Of course I brought it with me!* Then, because I wasn't completely insane...yet, I put on the matching panties.

I opened my adjoining door and knocked on his.

No answer.

He really is avoiding me.

I almost lost my nerve. But I reached for the door knob. It turned. Then I remembered. I was the last one to use the door last night, and *I didn't lock it.*

Try avoiding me now, Lance...

I hesitantly opened the door and looked around. *He's going to kill me for this.* I *wasn't* going to get lucky, and I *was* going to lose my job.

This was incredibly dumb. It was like going to Las Vegas and putting your life's savings on red.

I couldn't help it. This was the last night of the trip, and the way things were going, there wouldn't be another trip in my future. It was now or never.

I quietly walked in and closed the door behind me. He sat in a chair with his back toward me. He must have heard me, but he didn't flinch.

"What are you doing, Katie?"

Chapter 8

The Big One

"I-I knocked. But you didn't hear me."

"I heard you."

Oy. That was harsh.

As I drew closer, I noticed that he had a large sketch pad on his lap, and he was drawing a man's face with a charcoal pencil.

The face was similar to Lance's, but its shape was rounder. The man had dimples, and his eyes weren't as large and striking as Lance's were.

"Is that your brother?" I asked as I stood over him.

He grunted but otherwise ignored my question.

Wow. He's an artist, and a good one at that. Is there anything this man can't do?

And then it hit me.

"You painted the picture that's hanging in your office?"

He grunted again. He hardly acknowledged me. Instead, he continued working on his sketch.

I looked at the end table situated next to his chair, on which sat a round glass with unfinished brandy in it.

"Sake wasn't working fast enough?"

"Not really," he answered without looking at me.

But I was still relieved that his reply contained words instead of a grunt.

I knelt down beside the chair and leaned over the arm rest.

"Come on, Lance. We were having a good day."

No response. The only thing I heard was the pencil rubbing against the paper.

"I can understand you not wanting a party. But don't you at least want some company on your birthday?"

"No."

"Why not? And please stop drawing for two seconds so that we can talk."

Before he could respond, because I knew he probably wouldn't, I asked, "What's up with your brother anyway?"

His pencil froze.

"Why are you sitting in a room all alone drawing his picture?"

His eyes found mine, and now he did look like a lost little boy.

"What's the story, Lance?"

He placed the pad and pencil on the floor.

After he straightened up, he replied, "He died fifteen years ago."

I kinda figured. He had talked about him in past tense.

With his pad out of the way, I noticed that he sat there in navy boxers and nothing else. Considering the subject of our conversation, he looked even more vulnerable in his state of undress.

"I'm so sorry Lance. I don't know what to say."

He draped his arm around me and gently stroked my hair. His other hand reached for the glass of brandy, and he took a sip.

I inhaled sharply. "Why are you thinking about that now?"

His eyes found mine. "Thursday was the anniversary of his death."

Oh God. "So that's what you and your mom were doing?"

He nodded. "We flew to Washington. We visited the gravesites of Tim and my dad. They're buried side-by-side at Arlington National Cemetery."

Wow. I can hardly move. I didn't know if I should leave after hearing that, or if he really did need some company. But for right now, the brandy wasn't talking back to him, so I decided to stay.

"The wrong brother survived," he said in his monotone voice as he put the brandy glass down.

It felt like lightning had hit me straight through the heart. *How could he say something like that? How could he possibly think that his life has no value?*

I hadn't known him for long, but Lance was one of the most amazing men that I had ever met. He had accomplished a lot in his lifetime.

I knew that it must be hard for him. I had lost a family member too. But to want to switch places with his brother? That was just heartbreaking.

A tear welled up in my eye. I couldn't completely feel his pain, but what I felt was painful enough.

I stood and sat on his lap. I wrapped my arms around his neck and curled up against him.

He didn't move. I don't think he knew how to react. But then he slowly wrapped his arms around me and pulled me into a firm embrace.

"Katie, please don't cry. I don't know how I can take it if you cry."

I couldn't see him. I had tucked my head under his chin. But I felt his strong hand stroke my hair again. *That must be comforting to him in some way.*

"How could you say something like that?" I trembled against his chiseled chest.

"You don't even know me."

That did it. I pulled away far enough so that I could look him in the eyes. "You're right. I don't know you."

Then I climbed off his lap, grabbed the brandy glass and gulped down its contents.

Boy...was that nasty!

"But I think you're special enough that I want to get to know you." I slammed the glass back down on the end table.

His eyes shifted toward mine. "I thought you didn't drink."

I put my hand on my hip. "Someone had to stop you from your little binge."

"Do I sound drunk?"

"No...which is actually pretty scary. How high is your tolerance?"

"High enough. Now, I'm assuming you didn't come in here dressed like that so that we could talk."

Eep! After everything that he just said, I was embarrassed about my little stunt. *But I guess it's too late now!*

"I'm sorry. I really had no idea what to expect when I got here."

"Don't worry. It covers up more than that bathing suit did."

"You really didn't like it, did you?"

His tiny smile actually returned. *Yay!*

"I liked it just fine. But you do realize that I'm not blind, right?"

"Huh?"

"You don't have to go to so much trouble to get me to notice you."

I stood there motionless. "What do you mean?"

"To answer your question from before, I do find you attractive. Even when you're fully clothed."

I still can't move. I observed Lance in the chair. Those boxers didn't cover up much. The man was all washboard abs, attached to muscular thighs. My imagination went crazy thinking about what he could do with those legs.

Then my eyes wandered to the door that connected our two rooms. Logically, I should have walked out and left him alone. He had been drinking, and he was depressed. I didn't want to take advantage of him like this.

"I should go." I uttered as I took a step toward my room.

But then I heard the creak of the seat cushion as Lance rose from his chair.

I faced him, and a smoldering expression lit his features. "I'm not naïve either. I've known how you felt. I've known it all along."

Oh hell. Now I really need to leave.

He closed the distance between us. "We've been flirting Katie, and it's my fault."

I looked him straight in the eyes at this point. But my breathing had stopped.

"You make me feel important."

His fingertips brushed the bottom seam of my nighty. "Do you always sleep in something like this?"

"Sometimes I sleep in nothing at all." I breathed.

His hand caressed my back. "Is that so?"

I wrapped my arms around his neck. "Mmhmm."

"You know...we really shouldn't be doing this," Lance advised.

"I know."

Did he really think that comment was going to stop me?

I captured his lips, and I wasn't letting go this time.

It was a desperate kiss, a wanton kiss. A kiss that seemed to last until my breath was completely exhausted. I ran my hand up and down his washboard abs, as my tongue massaged his. With my other hand, I laced my fingers through his silky, black hair.

The kiss ended, as my legs trembled with a singular aching need. Lance caught me and pressed my body to his. Only a thin layer of silk kept my breasts from melting into his muscular chest. The hard evidence of his affection below my waist startled me, and I nearly lost my balance once more.

He looked me in the eyes. "Katie, this changes everything. Are you sure you really want this?"

I nodded breathlessly. I had never wanted anything more in my entire life.

"No regrets?" he asked.

I struggled out, "No regrets."

He slipped his arm under my legs and picked me up bridal-style. He carried me to the bedroom and laid me gently on the bed. This not being what I had in mind, I slid to my knees on the floor and petitioned him with my eyes to lie down.

Momentarily confused, he then obliged.

I slid my fingers into the waistband of his boxers and glimpsed at his bewildered face. "I want to give you a memory of your birthday that you'll want to remember always."

I slowly pulled his boxer shorts down. His stiff cock impeded my progress, but I maneuvered around it, and the pads of my fingertips traced the muscles of his legs as I removed the offending garment.

I could see his large organ even in the darkness. The thought of giving him a blow job suddenly provoked my gag reflexes. I certainly could not take all of him into my mouth.

But that didn't stop me. I pulled off my nighty before I climbed on top of him. I wanted to feel his strong thighs against my bare breasts.

I settled in between his legs and soon had the whole of his manhood in my mouth, much to my own surprise. I sucked his rod, using the tip of my tongue to massage the seam below the swollen crown. I licked the length of his shaft at my leisure, and my tongue idly found its way back to the glans of his penis.

I took his shaft with my right hand and grasped his balls with my left. I pumped the shaft, while licking it with the flat of my tongue, like an ice cream cone. I soon took the head back into my mouth.

He moaned, and shifted his head to the side, causing locks of pitch-black hair to spill over his porcelain-white face.

I continued my ministrations, and his hips bucked. I knew he was enjoying himself. But I wanted to get him off. I let the tip of my tongue taste the hole at the top of his head and trickle down to the seam. Then I traced back up to the top. I alternated between this and sucking the head. Then I used my lips to further massage underneath the crown.

All of a sudden, he pulled me into his arms. *Oh God, this wasn't a part of the plan!*

"I want to make you come too." He managed to struggle out through his heavy breathing.

"I really don't mind."

"I do."

He tugged at the string on the side of my black panties.

"Why are these still on?"

He immediately freed me of my panties. The sudden exposure between my legs sent a shiver up my spine.

He positioned me over his hard member. Then he placed it directly below my opening. I closed my eyes, and with a deep breath, I took him inside me.

I was wet, so I easily accommodated him. He put his hands on my waist to lift me up, and I was pulled back only to thrust down a little deeper.

He filled me up, and I felt the room spinning. It was all I could do to keep breathing. I positioned my hips so that I could take him in as deep as possible and then lifted up again. He guided me with his hands, and each time I went down, I went faster and harder. Inside me, he touched just the right spot, and I could feel the tension build in my stomach.

"Faster," I begged.

"I'm not going to last much longer."

I couldn't even register what he had just said. From what he was doing to me, I didn't care. Nothing else mattered.

"I'm so close," I said breathlessly.

He didn't verbally answer me, but he obliged by helping me go faster. It only took a few more thrusts before I felt the vibrations shake throughout my body.

God. I had never had an orgasm quite like that one. I sweated, and my heart pounded. I struggled to catch my breath.

Since Lance guided me with his hands, the thrusting did not stop. I felt a few more hard, quick thrusts, and then he groaned. His arms dropped, and he turned his head while his heavy breathing continued.

I collapsed and put my arms around his chest. He sweated too. I positioned myself so that he would stay inside me. I wanted that feeling to last for as long as possible.

After a few minutes of holding each other, he whispered in my ear, "Let's go get washed up."

"Do you want to go first?"

"Let's go together."

Huh? But I didn't have time to think about it. He gently rolled me off of him, so he could stand. Then he took me by the hand and led me to the bathroom.

His bathroom was *nice*. It had a large circular Jacuzzi tub and a separate shower. He turned the water on at the tub.

Hmm...what is he planning? Whatever it was, it seemed interesting.

When the tub was half full, he motioned with his hand. "Get in."

"Okay..."

I stepped into the tub and sat down.

He placed his hand on my shoulder. "Scoot over."

He planned to sit behind me. *Interesting.*

I wondered what he had in mind. I had seen how much he loved the pool. I guess I shouldn't have been surprised that the man had a water fetish.

He sat down and pulled me back so that I was flush against his body. I could feel his dick pressed up against my ass. It wasn't hard...yet.

The warm water had almost filled the tub when his hands found their way to my breasts. He took my nipples between his fingers and pinched.

Between his hands on my nipples and his growing dick touching my ass, I started to lose my mind again.

He turned off the water. Then he nuzzled his head on my shoulder.

Before I knew it, his hand was back on my breast. His lips clamped down onto my neck, just below my earlobe. It hurt, but at the same time, it felt so good. He sucked and kneaded my breasts. He rubbed them, one and then the other, and then both at the same time. He blew on my neck and then used the tip of his tongue to swirl around the swollen area.

He marked me as his own, and he drove me crazy while doing it. But I didn't mind in the least. I just didn't want his ministrations to stop. How did he know that area on my neck was one of my hot buttons?

I breathed heavily as I turned to him. There was one thing that I had wanted to do for the longest time.

I kissed along his jaw line, as my hand took hold of his shaft. I slowly pumped him up and down, while my kisses traced his jaw line from his left ear to his right. Then I gently nibbled the jaw line on my way back to his left ear.

Was it the warm water...or just me? I was sweating again. How could I be this turned on so quickly after our last encounter? But I was also proud of myself. I was finally nibbling his jaw line! *Took me long enough.*

I was still stroking his dick when I felt his hand between my legs. He used his index finger to circle my clit.

I could hardly concentrate on what I was doing to him. I couldn't keep kissing him. I struggled to breathe. I tilted my head so that I could look him straight in the eyes. And he smiled, devilishly this time.

He whirled me back around and positioned my ass so that his hard dick could enter me again. I pressed him in, and I could hear him groan from behind me. I could imagine him closing his eyes as he made that sexy sound.

I took him in deeper. He captured my breasts with both hands to hold me steady. I thrusted up and down in short, hard intervals. The room spun again. Then I felt him finger my clit. *Oh, my God.* I couldn't take it. The pleasurable sensations came from too many directions. His hand on my breast, his dick inside me, and now the swirling sensation on my clit were all bringing me to the edge. To make matters worse, he bit down on the base of my neck.

I was losing it, and fast. He let go of my breast and clit momentarily so that he could position my hips to penetrate me even deeper. I thrust a few more times and...

There it was.

"Oh Lance!" I screamed.

My body jerked a few times, and I could feel the walls of my vagina clamp on and off of his dick. He groaned and took a firmer hold of my waist. He moved me up and down and shifted his hips for added friction, and then I felt him pulse inside of me. He exhaled heavily and laid his head on my shoulder.

He was still inside me. And it felt so good. I wanted to stay connected to him. It felt like heaven, and I had no intention of returning to Earth any time soon.

We remained in that position. His head nuzzled my shoulder. His arms cradled me against his chest.

I felt no need to rush out of his arms. In those peaceful moments, I finally felt the real Lance. There was a gentleness to him that I had never seen in another guy. And it made me want him even more.

I turned my head and said, "You really are a cuddler."

I felt him straighten a little. "Is that bad?"

"No. It's very good." I settled myself so that I was deeper in his embrace.

I could feel him lean closer to me too.

He sat there for a moment and then said, "I like how this feels."

It's his birthday, and he obviously likes being touched. I have an idea!

"Would you like a massage?"

"What type of massage?" he inquired in an accusing tone.

"Not that kind! A back massage."

"Oh. Right now?"

"Um, when would you like it?"

"In a couple of minutes. I'm enjoying holding you like this," he murmured in my ear.

I placed my arms over his. "I don't mind it, either."

We sat there for a while, and then Lance reluctantly got out of the tub. As he rose out of the water, he looked like a well-oiled marble statue of a Greek God. He was nothing but muscle from head to toe.

He offered his hand, and I took it. I saw his eyes as he stared at me when I stood. I guess we hadn't had the chance to really survey each other's naked bodies in the heat of passion. But now, in the light of the bathroom, we could see what once was hidden.

I saw a bottle of lotion on the bathroom counter and grabbed it. The lotion wasn't exactly massage oil, but it would have to do in a pinch. I was lucky that we were staying in a nice hotel that supplied that sort of thing.

We walked to the bedroom and to his bed. I told him to lie down. He did, and then I noticed his butt staring at me. That was definitely getting massaged first.

I sat on his thighs and rubbed my hands together. I wanted them to be as warm as they could be. Usually I used warm massage oil, but that wasn't available at the moment. I poured some lotion in my hands and rubbed circles over his buttocks. They were tight and muscular. There was no fat to be found.

I sprinkled the lotion on his back and applied long, warm strokes from top to bottom. Then I worked my way up. First, I concentrated on the small of his back, applying pressure where I found knots. Then I massaged his mid-section and shoulder blades.

When I got to his neck, I found the stress points. All the muscles along his neck and shoulders were so tight that I could hardly work them out. I kneaded and rubbed the knotted muscles until my fingers got sore. His skin was kinda red from my efforts.

When I gave up and climbed off of him, he turned his head to look at me.

Then he flipped over onto his back and breathed out, "Come here."

I obliged and climbed over to his left side.

He pulled me into a warm embrace. I wrapped my arm around his waist and nuzzled my head against his chest.

I could hear his heartbeat. I could feel it. And his warmth invaded all of my senses and logic. It was soothing. It was calming. And despite myself, I started to drift to sleep.

As he held me there in bed, I felt wanted. I felt desired. And I hadn't felt that way in a very long time.

I never wanted to let him go.

≈•≈

Sunday, August 26, 2012 - 7:30 a.m.

The next day, I woke up first. I lifted my head off of his chest to get a better look at him. I couldn't believe it. I hadn't thought that he could ever get more beautiful. His hair was slightly messed up, thanks to me. But he looked so peaceful. Like an angel.

I just stared at his closed eyes. I had never noticed before, but I really liked his eyelashes and eyebrows. His eyebrows formed a thin line over that stunning pair of eyes. His eyelashes were long and thick. Both were black, like his hair, and served as the perfect contrast to frame his closed white eyelids. The man looked like someone had painted him according to a fairy tale's expectations.

He must have felt my stare because those black eyelashes fluttered. He opened his dark brown eyes and looked at me.

"Good morning sunshine," I said with a cheesy grin.

He gave me that tiny little smile of his. "Good morning."

Then he got up.

There is that Adonis-looking body of his again. Damn, I never get tired of looking at it!

He went straight to the bathroom without saying another word.

When he came out, I asked, "So, what do you want to do this morning?"

He gave me an uncomforting look. "Katie. We have a plane to catch."

"Yeah?" *Um, that wasn't the reaction I was expecting.*

He put on his clothes, so I sat up and wrapped the covers around me. "Do you think we'll be doing this again sometime?"

"We'll see," he answered.

Chapter 9

Denial

Oh God. We'll see equals you're fired. Well, it was good while it lasted.

He looked at me and said, "It's too late now, but I'm sorry I didn't wear a condom. I didn't have any. I wasn't prepared for last night."

I pulled my knees up to my chest, with the blankets still covering all the necessary areas. "That's okay, Lance. I'm on the pill. It's not a problem."

"You are?"

"I never go off of it. It throws my body out of whack when I stop taking the prescription."

"Oh, okay."

He didn't ask, but I felt the sudden urge to explain. "Lance, I don't do this all the time. I haven't had a boyfriend in quite a while. And I really like you."

I didn't blame him for wondering about me. We hadn't discussed it, and I did just seduce him after only one week of knowing him.

He quirked his eyebrow up at me. "You said you loved me after I gave you crème brulee, and now you *like* me after last night?"

I just stared at him. Was he trying to be funny, or was he really serious?

"You said you loved me for calling you sir."

Which, by the way, would be mega-weird to call you after last night...

He nodded in acknowledgment and said, "I'll leave. Why don't you get dressed and then go over to your room and get packed."

I didn't say a word. I was struck speechless, which was very rare for me. But this wasn't the morning after that I had expected.

But what had I expected? He had never made me any promises.

Was this the relationship that I had to look forward to? How could I possibly face this man, day in and day out, if this was the way he would act around me?

As soon as he left, I got out of his bed and picked up my nighty and panties. I stared at them and wondered if I had made a monumental mistake. It had seemed like such a good idea at the time. But now? I wasn't so sure.

I went to my room and closed the door. I didn't want to see him. At least, not for now.

But I couldn't escape him forever. A knock sounded on the front door of my room at 8:30 a.m.

When I didn't answer immediately, Lance called out, "Katie, the taxi's here."

I picked up my bag and opened the door. As I expected, he had a stone cold expression on his face. I followed him to the elevator in silence.

As we were going down, he offered to take my bag. I told him that I could handle it. What I didn't tell him was that I *couldn't* handle how he was treating me. *But I guess I brought it on myself.*

The drive to the airport was painfully silent. I almost wished that we had taken separate cabs. It was awkward. Neither of us knew what to say. I almost told him that I was sorry for what had happened between us. But I didn't know if that would bother him more.

While we waited for our plane, he went to get coffee for me. I guess that was nice of him, especially since he doesn't drink it. But all I could think while he was doing it was that it was his way of saying: *I'm sorry. I can't stand you anymore since we had sex, so here's your booby prize.* I didn't drink a sip of the coffee. I would rather have choked on it first.

We got on the plane and sat next to each other. This time I was *not* snuggled up next to him. He tried to pass the time by going over the information for Dr. Floyd and discussing the necessary steps to implementing his recommended portfolio. But I wasn't listening. I was going over last night in my mind and trying to figure out what had happened to make Lance act this way.

I seduced him. Yes I did. I take full responsibility for that. But I didn't twist his arm. He could have let me go back to my room.

And he certainly seemed to be enjoying himself at the time.

That flight was the longest six hours of my life. I wanted to fall asleep, but I would be damned if I was going to lean on Lance's shoulder this time. I was in the middle seat again, and on my other side was an older lady. Well, I wasn't going to lean on her, either! So I sat there, uncomfortable, until it was all over.

I couldn't wait to get home.

But what was there to go home to? When I got there, I just stared at the four walls. They refused to talk to me. Didn't they know that I was hurting? Didn't anyone know?

I had always been somewhat of a loner. So I didn't know why this bothered me so much. It was a one-night stand. I should have known it going in. But something was happening in my heart that I had not expected.

I didn't know what I had done wrong. Well, I *did* know what I had done *wrong*. But I couldn't figure out why he was so mad about it.

Why did I even care? I was hoping that sex would get him out of my system. I thought that this attraction was purely physical. But now, I couldn't get him off my mind. I seriously had feelings for him, but I couldn't decide whether those feelings were love or hate. Either way, they were very strong feelings. And I needed to purge them as soon as possible.

Working with the man would be nothing but awkward. I knew that. So I decided to text him so that we could discuss the situation:

Can we talk about last night – please?

The company monitors my texts.

I don't really care.

See. Two can play at that game.

But no further texts came back from him.

That didn't go well. But it didn't stop me. I called his cell, and when he didn't pick up, I decided to leave him a message:

Lance, a lot has happened between us. I think you'll agree. So please don't shut down on me again. I know how you are. It's your signature move. But I don't want to play that game with you anymore.

I hung up the phone and waited. I figured that he could take the next step.

And he didn't.

Chapter 10

Separation

Monday, August 27, 2012 - 8:00 a.m.

The next morning, I arrived at work right on time without a moment to spare. As I expected, Alyssa and Julie waited for me to hear details of the trip.

What should I say? I couldn't say what had *actually* happened. So I lied. I told them that it was incredibly boring and that I wasn't in the mood for any more trips. They weren't surprised. Alyssa told me that Lance had actually said the same thing in the past.

I told Maria what Lance had said about implementing our recommendations for Dr. Floyd's portfolio. Or at least, what I could remember through trying to ignore Lance during our flight. She nodded and started to work. She had the proposal, so she already had a good idea of what she needed to do.

Then I slumped down at my desk. I wanted to go home and not face the rest of the day. What was I going to do when Lance came in? *He ignored me last night. Should I ignore him today?*

Well, is it a good idea to ignore your boss? Probably not. But it wasn't a good idea to sleep with him, either. So as long as I'm breaking the rules, I might as well do so with gusto!

Before I could totally devise my plan, large-and-balding invaded my personal space.

"Where's Hardy?" he asked sternly.

I looked at him, and I'm sure I appeared disturbed.

This time, I put my hand in front of me, in an effort to make him step back, and said, "I don't know. I haven't heard from him yet."

He didn't seem to appreciate me protecting my personal space.

He looked at me with burning eyes. "Didn't you see him yesterday? What did he say?"

"What did he say about what, Mr. Biggerstaff?"

"When is he coming in?" He huffed.

"Doesn't he come in around 10:00?"

"Fuck! I'll call him on his cell." He stomped away.

Wow. He didn't sound happy. And anything that could tick Lance off even more was not a good thing.

I needed to come up with a plan, and fast.

To pass the time, I decided to help Marlene with some mailers that she was sending out. She appreciated the help but still didn't smile. It was a shame. I was sure she'd be pretty if she smiled.

As for Lance, instead of arriving early like he had last week, he got to the office at 10:30.

He passed by my desk and muttered, "Katie."

He didn't even look in my direction for an instant.

I wasn't going to take that. *Not this time.*

I left my stack of envelopes and followed him into his office. I made sure to close the door behind me. He looked surprised at first.

But then he composed himself and said, "Not now. I'm busy."

"Sure you are."

"I am." Anger showed on his face. "I have to call one of Led's bigger clients. He's irate, and I'm better at calming him down than Led is."

"That's interesting. Because you aren't the least bit good at calming me down."

"That's different."

"How?"

He sighed. "Katie, do we really need to do this now?"

"If not now, when?" I asked.

My arm rested on my hip, and I aggressively leaned toward him.

"During lunch. We'll go out and talk. But for now, I really have to call this client." He took a deep breath. "Besides, I don't want you yelling at me in my own office. I don't need the other girls hearing this conversation."

"I don't care." I had started to like the *I don't care* mantra of Lance's.

It had helped me out twice now.

"But I do." He turned his chair to face his computer. "We'll talk at lunch."

Damn him. I was dismissed, and it didn't make me very happy. I didn't know if I should walk out or just strangle him. But I decided to walk out for now and strangle him later.

I went back to my desk and tried to work on the mailer. But who was I kidding? I spent more time looking at the clock than stuffing envelopes. The clock *s-l-o-w-l-y* ticked its way to noon. It was excruciating.

Lance never left his office. I didn't even have a chance to sneer at him while I waited.

That is...until Stacy waltzed by me and right into his office at precisely 12:00.

She didn't close the door, so I was anxious to hear what he would tell her. But I heard nothing. There was no yelling and no tears.

And then the two of them walked out of his office... Together.

I watched as they passed me, with my mouth wide open. Words would have failed me in expressing my emotions. I glared at Lance, but he ignored me. He didn't even give me the slightest look of remorse.

I knew that she was supposedly his girlfriend. I got that. But today was *my* day. We needed to get rid of the two thousand pound elephant in the room. The tension between us was stifling. And we needed to decide if we were going to part as friends or as enemies.

But it became abundantly clear that we were going to part, one way or the other.

Coward! How could he just walk out like that? Well, I'd be damned if I was going to just sit back and wait anymore. We were going to talk when he got back.

His lunch hour seemed to last forever. I didn't even *pretend* to stuff envelopes while he was gone. And I didn't help Maria cover the phones, which was wrong of me. She didn't cause the problem, yet she had to suffer for it.

If I had been watching the clock before, then I was completely mesmerized by it now. It moved even slower knowing that Lance was with his *girlfriend*. I hoped that the two of them would choke on their lunch.

He came back alone. Good thinking on his part. He tried to walk back to his office without talking to me, but it didn't work. I followed him. I stormed into his office and slammed the door. I slammed it so hard that I was surprised I didn't shatter the glass.

"What the fuck was that?" I hissed at him.

He sat down and looked at me with a blank expression. "What was what?"

"Don't play stupid. It doesn't become you. Didn't you say that *we* were going to have lunch?"

"Stacy came by. What was I supposed to do?"

"Tell her to fuck off."

"She's my girlfriend. Why would I do that?"

"You're still going out with her? After everything that happened? You don't even like her."

He sat there for a second.

I could tell that he was trying to figure out exactly how to say his next line. "I never promised to break up with her."

I was shocked. Of course he was right.

But, for some illogical reason, I had hoped that this would end up differently. "I just thought..."

"I didn't tell you to seduce me."

That hurt.

I stood there stunned. What could I possibly say after that? I looked at him, and then, I looked at the picture on his wall.

His mother holding his brother. The two most important people in Lance's life.

One died, and the other moved away. *Is that why Lance finds it so difficult to express intimacy?*

The picture called out to me, as if it was a glimpse into Lance's soul.

And why was it a picture of just his mother and brother? Why did he not paint himself and his father around them?

My gaze shifted back to his large, almond-shaped eyes. "Where is your father in that picture?"

That took him aback. But as usual, he composed himself pretty quickly.

"Nowhere."

I narrowed my eyes at him. "Lance, why not?"

I wasn't going for vague at the moment, and I was showing him through my expression and stance that I wanted the truth for once.

"He never gave a shit about me."

Oh fuck. I could have guessed. None of the artwork that I had seen had depicted his dad's image. And he had just visited his dad's gravesite along with his brother's.

Then, he readily told me that his dad had passed away without any emotion at all. I had to drag it out of him that he even had a brother.

But...Lance just cussed. He didn't do that often. *He's getting riled up too.*

My brain decided to shut down and let my mouth run amok. I guessed that my ego needed a way to out-trump him before he had the chance to get really angry and say something to mortally wound me.

"That makes a whole lot of sense. Your dad would be very proud of you right now. Because you don't give a shit about anyone else, either."

I could see the hurt expression on his face.

But he kept the tone of his voice steady. "I'm sorry you feel that way. What exactly have I done to make you think so low of me?"

"You've shut me out, like you do to everybody."

He put his head in his hands and rubbed his temples. "Katie. I really don't have the time or energy for this right now."

Then he turned to face his computer. "Get the hell out of my office."

He cussed at me again. And this time he told me to leave. But for some reason, my legs wouldn't move. And I didn't know how to respond.

It took me a minute. He didn't turn back to look at me again. I slowly started to feel like a stooge just standing there. So I turned and stomped out of his office.

And when I came out, three pairs of very stunned eyes greeted me. *Oh God,* my slamming the door earlier alerted everyone in the office that Lance and I were arguing.

"What happened?" Alyssa asked.

"He's a jackass."

"We know that. But that's never bothered you before," Julie quipped.

I wasn't in the mood. I trudged to my desk and slumped in my chair.

Maria motioned to the others. "Come on. Let's leave her alone."

I was thankful that Maria got everyone to leave.

But now I was alone, and I felt it. I didn't know what to do. My nerves were completely shot, and I needed to take my aggression out on something. I sat there, stared at the computer screen, and thought about everything that had happened.

I hurt Lance by what I had said. And that's why I said it.

I don't know what I was thinking.

Why did I care? I *wanted* to hurt him, like he was hurting me. I *wanted* him to feel my pain. But was it completely fair? I brought this on, and now I was punishing him for it.

But he didn't have to go along with it. He had a choice. And now both of us have to live with the decisions we made that night.

Still, what had happened between us had been so beautiful. It meant so much to me. And it didn't seem like he felt the same way. I guess that's what hurt the most. I thought there was a connection that was much stronger than the physical act. *I guess I was wrong.*

I felt like a complete and total idiot. *Why did I have to go into his room that night?*

Deep down inside, I knew that none of this was his fault. He didn't ask for this. He had tried to persuade me against it. And I didn't listen. But somehow, I still couldn't help but feel completely betrayed.

I couldn't take it anymore. I picked up my bag, didn't even bother to log off of my computer, and plodded over to Maria's desk.

"I'm gone for the day."

I started to turn and head for the front door, but then I heard Maria's quiet voice from behind me. "Will you be back tomorrow?"

I stood there motionless for a second.

Then, without looking back at her, I responded, "I don't know."

I left the office as quickly as my legs could take me.

Chapter 11

~✌~

Shattered

Tuesday, August 28, 2012 - 7:30 a.m.

Tuesday morning, I woke up. But I knew that I wasn't going to work. What was there to go back to exactly? I knew that I would never accompany Lance on any more of his trips. It would be too painful. So what was I supposed to do when that part of my job was now impossible?

Maria did admin, Alyssa did proposals, Julie did customer service, and Lance was the sales guy. There was absolutely no need for me at all.

At 8:30, the phone rang. I knew it couldn't be Lance. He probably didn't even know that I was absent yet.

"Hello," I answered.

"Hey." It was Maria. It figured.

When I didn't say anything, she continued, "How are you feeling today?"

"Not good."

"I see." She hesitated, but then asked, "Will you be coming back? Lance wants to know."

That's a surprise. How did he even realize I wasn't there? It wasn't close to 10:00 yet.

Maria must have called him.

And...he was too gutless to call me himself.

That actually made me angrier. He must have known how much I respected Maria. So why did he send her to do his dirty work? That was low, even for him.

"Tell him to fuck himself."

"Can I paraphrase?" Maria sounded uncomfortable.

I felt bad for putting her in this position. But actually it was *Lance* who had put her in this position, not me.

"No, you can't." And I hung up the phone.

That was totally unfair. Maria hadn't done anything to deserve being hung up on. I would have to apologize to her later. What I had wanted to do was hang up on Lance. But *he* didn't give me the chance.

The rest of the day, I sulked. I was screwed, and I knew it. In more ways than one. And the worst part about it? I had brought it all on myself.

I didn't have a boyfriend. I didn't have a job. But I *did* have bills to pay.

I was too depressed to think about it.

So I sat, all day, in my pajamas. I tried to watch soap operas, but since I didn't know what was going on, I ended up flipping through the channels. I took out a carton of chocolate ice cream, hoping that by eating it, somehow, magically, it would make me feel better.

It didn't. This problem transcended the power of chocolate ice cream.

I had nowhere to go and nothing to do. The internet wasn't interesting. I didn't really have any friends. I tried to go to sleep, but I ended up tossing and turning.

I literally drove myself right into a migraine. I started getting nauseated, and my head was full of sharp pain. I took a warm bath and tried to stomach some high-powered migraine medicine. But I threw it up.

I was miserable. Depression and migraines together were worse than death. I was sprawled next to the toilet in the bathroom, cheek against the cold bathroom floor, and couldn't move. If I lifted my head, I felt nauseated again. That chocolate ice cream was really not a good idea.

Some of the medicine must have worked somehow, as I felt tired after about an hour. I thanked God for his mercy. I crawled into bed and threw the covers over me. I felt chilled, but at least the spinning and nausea started to subside. After that, I slowly drifted off to sleep.

⚹

Wednesday, August 29, 2012 - 8:00 a.m.

I woke up and decided to pull myself together. I got dressed and went out to find a newspaper. It was time to start looking for a job. I briefly wondered if I would qualify for unemployment. But then I glimpsed the application in my mind's eye. Reason for termination: *Slept with the boss.*

Hmm...maybe not.

Surprisingly, I didn't receive a phone call from the office. *I guess Lance finally gave up.* It was the right decision on his part. Why continue torturing everyone involved? It was time for the whole team to move on with their lives.

I scanned the help-wanted ads in the newspaper. Nothing seemed to pop out at me. Then I started looking at online postings.

What a surprise! My old job was listed.

As depressed as I was, I knew I wasn't *that* desperate. Knowing that bitch-o-rama had to answer her own phones lifted my mood.

I searched the rest of the postings, and nothing else matched my expertise. I could be a secretary, but it wouldn't pay as well as my old job had. The only reason that I had gotten a bump up in salary was because I was securities licensed. Outside of the financial services industry, that designation wasn't worth a damn.

I looked away from the computer in disgust. *How did my life get so freakin' complicated? What did I ever do to deserve this?*

Well...besides sleeping with the boss...

My life, up to this point, had been a never-ending revolving door of unhappiness.

Mom was an alcoholic, and that made it mighty hard to hold down a job. We did not live in the lap of luxury. As a matter of fact, mom would have loved to live as nice as I do now, even though I am definitely on the lower end of the money scale. I wouldn't even classify myself as middle class.

But I didn't live on assistance, and that was a nice bonus.

When I was young, men came and went out of my mother's life. Not a single one stuck around for long. There was definitely no one that I could have called a father. I didn't even grasp what that word meant.

I wonder what really happened between Lance and his father. It had to be better than having no father at all.

A couple of the men tried to get touchy-feely with me. I wasn't having that. I guess that's where I developed my personal space issues. I had to establish my boundaries at an early age to protect myself.

Toward the end, mom became suicidal. It was tough on her, and it was extremely hard on me. I was her self-appointed protector and had to stop her on several occasions. She ended up at the hospital more times than I could remember. It got to be a routine that I could hardly bear.

After high school, I attended community college. But one day after class, I got home, and Mom was drunk. Like usual.

She was slumped over on the couch. She saw me and looked into my eyes. Her eyes were crossed, and she was so far beyond being mentally there.

She sang, "You are my sunshine, my only sunshine."

After a few choruses, she looked me in the eyes again. "I love you Katie."

I shook my head. "Mom."

Our roles had always been reversed. It seemed that I had always been the one to take care of her like a child. So I wrapped her arm around my shoulder. I slowly dragged her back to the bedroom. When we got there, I laid her flat on her back and then left the room to study. She was unconscious at that point, so I wanted her to sleep it off.

A few hours later, I decided to check on her. Don't ask me why. Maybe it was intuition.

I found her unresponsive.

The ambulance came, and the paramedic told me that it was too late. She had been gone for a while. He said that she must have vomited and choked, since she laid flat on her back.

I replayed that day over and over in my mind. I felt guilty as hell for laying her flat on her back. But how could I have known?

How ironic? She tried to commit suicide and never succeeded. She wasn't trying that time, or at least that I was aware of, and her body finally had enough.

After that, I shut myself off completely. I was never going to let someone else leave me like that again. Ever. And the only way to make sure that someone didn't leave was to never let them in.

Ever since then, I had been alone. And that's how I preferred it.

Now, I had royally fucked up. I knew that I had been right all along. I opened my heart to Lance. I should have known better.

After Mom died, I subconsciously picked boyfriends who I knew would hurt me. *I don't know why.* Did I really think that I needed to be punished for some reason? Logically, I knew that I wasn't responsible for my mother's death. And wherever she was now, I knew she was much happier. She had to be. But then why did I insist on making myself unhappy.

I wanted a man to call my own. One that would stay. But I didn't know how to go about finding one. Long-term relationships seemed to work for other people. But they had never worked out for Mom. And they had never worked out for me.

Then there was Lance.

I had indulged my desire for him. Now I was paying the price.

Whatever happened to my fairy tale? Where was the end of my rainbow? When would my knight in shining armor finally arrive?

⚜

Thursday, August 30, 2012 - 8:30 a.m.

I was tired of this whole depressed routine already. I didn't have any right to be mad, and I was starting to realize it. Lance had never asked for any of this. I had forced it on him. And now, I sat here fuming because he wasn't going along with plans that he had no part in formulating in the first place.

Was I truly this selfish? I was seriously becoming ashamed of myself and my actions. Now I did have to quit, if I happened to still have a job. This time it wasn't because of something *he* had done. It was because I just couldn't face him again.

I had intentionally hurt him before I left the office. It was a low blow to compare him to his father. It was obviously a sore subject, and I dragged it out of him and then went for the throat.

That wasn't the person that I wanted him to see. I wanted to show him that I cared for him. I wanted to show him how much our night together had meant to me. But instead, all I showed him was my bad side.

Furthermore, I was trying to make Lance into something he wasn't. He was completely honest and upfront with me, and now I was mad at him for being right about the outcome.

No regrets. His words echoed in my mind. I had obviously lied to him big time.

We are supposed to love someone for who they are, not what we want them to be. When did I forget that?

The more I thought about it, the more I saw Lance for the man he truly was. I remembered massaging him that night, and I remembered how much he enjoyed just holding me in the tub. Then he held me all night long as we slept. His actions were not ones that came from being a heartless prick. He was gentle and kind. He was a good man, and I knew it.

And he was a man that seemed to harbor a lot of pain. Instead of trying to help him through it, I was just adding to it.

He also seemed to be very stressed. I remembered his knotted muscles and the fact that he wouldn't eat before a presentation because he said he might get sick. I thought about his white knuckles as he held his briefcase when we went to see Dr. Floyd. He said that he never got nervous, but his actions clearly said otherwise. And hiding it so well must be very taxing on him.

It seemed to me that with everything he did, he felt the need to be perfect. I guess that was how he got the position he did at his young age. The poor guy was always on. He never let go and just felt like he could be himself.

He was such a people pleaser, but he never stopped to try and please himself along the way.

So what did Lance really want? And would I ever find out?

The only time I saw him let go was at the pool and during the night we spent together. That was the real him that he never showed. And that was the man I wanted to be with.

I wanted to call and apologize. But my ego wouldn't let me. Besides, too much time had passed to play that card now. It was done.

But if I couldn't find happiness, then I wanted Lance to find his. He *was* a good guy. He made love to me that night because I wanted him to. Sure, he enjoyed it. But it was my idea, and he went along with it.

He didn't deserve the aftermath that followed.

⥲⋅⥲

Thursday, August 30, 2012 - 7:30 p.m.

There was a knock at the door. *Who could that be? I never have any visitors. And it couldn't be a delivery man or a solicitor. It's too late at night.*

Could it be Lance? Nah, he doesn't give a shit about me. Move on already.

But curiosity kept killing the cat.

So I opened the door.

Next thing I saw was a fist flying toward my face. Afterwards, I felt the pain of my hip and head crashing against the hardwood floor of my entranceway.

Chapter 12

Unexpected

Pain came from all directions. The fist had connected with the corner of my eye, so my vision was slightly blurry for the moment. The back of my head was developing a large bump, and my hip throbbed.

I was so disoriented that I didn't know if I was being mugged or what. But I tried to focus my eyes on the intruder.

It was a female... with red hair.

Oh hell. It's Stacy.

With an ice-cold glare, she said, "Did you have fun with Lance?"

Like I'm going to answer that! But I wasn't afraid of her. I had already beaten myself up harder than she ever could.

I didn't get up.

I just returned her stare. "Are you going to hit me again? Because I'd like to be prepared next time."

She stood there motionless. I imagined that she was trying to decide her next move.

But what could she do? Beating me up wouldn't change a thing. And she might just lose the fight if I was given half a chance.

"You can have him." She glowered at me, but then turned on her heel and left.

Her disappearing image in the dark hallway of my building was one of the most welcome sights of this entire week.

I got up and went to get an ice pack. *Damn, I need about two or three!* But I decided that the one ice pack I had needed to be directly on my eye. *Tomorrow I'll have a real shiner there.*

Hell. Lance must have told her what happened.

But why? Why would he tell her? Wouldn't it be better to keep the secret? I thought he wanted to stay with her.

And if he didn't...

Don't jump to conclusions. He hasn't reached out to me either.

That sneak attack was the perfect ending to my terrible week. I downed a couple of aspirin and took my icepack to bed with me. I just wanted to sleep and forget about the whole thing.

That is...if the bump on the back of my head would let me.

≈❖≈

Friday, August 31, 2012 - 9:00 a.m.

I tried to search through the help wanted ads, but I figured it would be better to wait until Sunday's paper. I had sent a couple of resumes to some online listings, but I hadn't heard anything back yet.

Besides, who wanted to go on a job interview with a black eye? I'm sure that would lead to some lovely questions.

And it would be uncomfortable enough as it already stood:

"Why did you leave your previous job?" My prospective employer would ask.

"Oh that? I just slept with the boss. That's all."

Choke. "Don't call us. We'll call you."

Fantastic. I think I'll wait until the black eye heals. Then I'll come up with a better answer to the previous job question.

I got dressed, barely. I didn't bother messing with my hair and make-up. My hair was brushed, but that was about it. Curly hair suited my mood better than the straight look that I usually wore when I went out.

I didn't bother covering up the black eye. I didn't care. I had done the deed, and now I was doing the time. It was like my personal version of *The Scarlet Letter A* that I decided to wear with pride.

I threw on my sweats and an old t-shirt and walked to the neighborhood deli for breakfast.

I hadn't gone shopping all week. Who had the energy? Beating yourself up takes a lot out of a person. So now I had no food, and unbelievably, I was hungry.

I don't know how long I was out. I wasn't keeping track. Who cared? I didn't have a job, and I had no one to be accountable to. So I could be out all day, doing absolutely nothing, if I wanted to.

I walked up the stairs to my apartment, and when I looked down the hallway, I saw a tall man standing at my door. As I got closer, I made out the navy blue business suit and silky black hair.

He was turned away from me. *Should I run in the opposite direction? What should I do?*

But my curiosity got the best of me again, so I kept walking toward him. He must have felt my presence because he turned around and looked at me with those large, dark-colored eyes of his.

"Katie."

"Hmm."

I walked up to my door and unlocked it.

"Can I come in?"

"That depends." I glared at him. "Are you here to punch me too?"

He gave me a confused look. But then he noticed my black eye.

His fingertips grazed the side of my face. "How did you get that?"

He's really surprised. I wonder why?

And he's touching me!

"Your lovely girlfriend gave it to me."

His eyes widened. "Why?"

"Isn't it obvious?"

He shook his head. "No. I meant...why would she do that to *you*? Why wouldn't she punch me? I'm the one who cheated on her."

"Lance, you would have been a heck of a lot harder to take down than I was."

He thought about it for a second and said, "I suppose you're right. I'm sorry that happened to you."

"I'm sure you are."

"I didn't want her to beat you up!" he exclaimed.

Lance was finally here, and now I'm fighting with him again. When will my mouth stop for just a second and listen to my brain?

"You told her," I muttered.

He stepped back and took a deep breath. "I thought that's what you wanted."

I did. I just didn't want to be sucker punched afterwards.

"Well, I hope she got her hostility out of her system."

He raised his eyebrow. "You know, you could press charges against her."

"And say what? I slept with her boyfriend and she decked me? No thank you. I'd rather not."

Lance drew closer to me. "I'm really sorry. But I didn't come here to talk about Stacy."

"Well, I didn't think we had anything else to talk about."

"I didn't walk out on you." He pointed out.

"No. You didn't. But you might as well have. Do you have any idea how it feels when someone you care about refuses to talk to you?"

He didn't answer. It seemed like he was allowing me to get it out of my system.

"You know what? Bite me." I opened the door, went inside, and tried to shut it in his face.

But he stopped the door with his hand. Dammit, the man was much stronger than I was. There was no way that I would win this particular battle.

"You want me to talk to you? Well, here I am."

I stood there and stared at him through the crack in the door.

It took me a second before I composed myself, but then I asked, "Why? Why now?"

"Do I have to do this out in the hallway?"

I smirked. "It kinda feels the same as when you throw me out of your office."

He looked down momentarily. I could tell he felt a little guilty.

But then he looked me straight in the eyes with those mesmerizing orbs of his. "I know. I'm sorry. Now can you please let me in so that I can apologize properly?"

He was here to apologize? I *had* to hear this. It should be good.

I opened the door but then looked around my apartment a little too late. I was a bit embarrassed. I had heard the girls say that he lived in downtown Manhattan. And here he was, standing in my studio apartment in Brooklyn. What an eye-opener this must be for him.

Besides, cleaning hadn't been at the top of my agenda for the last week. The apartment probably smelled like death. Because that was how I felt...

When Lance walked in, I saw him survey his surroundings. He didn't seem fazed.

He looked me in the eyes again and said, "Katie, I'm sorry for the way I acted. I didn't know how to handle what was going on between us. And I did give a shit about you, but I didn't know how to express it."

I put my hand on my hip. "So not talking to me seemed like the right thing to do?"

"No. I just didn't know what to say."

I almost exploded. "You could have said anything, and it would have been better than the way you treated me."

"I know that now." He took a deep breath and continued, "This must be my fate. I don't know what's wrong with me. Marlene won't talk to me either."

"You...slept...with Marlene?" I shrieked.

"Hell no. But I rejected her. She hasn't been the same since." His voice was as even as ever.

The man really could remain calm as people screamed in his face.

So that's what happened with Marlene. No wonder...

She hated me before, so now that hate has probably skyrocketed to supersonic level. It wouldn't take a brain surgeon to figure out why Lance and I fought. Most people don't storm out of a new job after spending the weekend with their hot boss.

Unless...

They fucked each other's brains out.

Or close to it...

First I took the job she wanted. Now I've slept with the man she had a thing for.

"Lance."

"Yes, Katie."

"Exactly when should I expect Marlene to come here and beat me up?"

"I didn't tell her," he asserted.

"Oh. Well, I guess that means that she and the others in the office are completely blind, deaf, and dumb?"

His tiny smile tugged at his lips. "There have been rumors."

"Rumors? Then how do you know about them? No one's going to tell you rumors about *you*."

"I have my ways."

Yep, he really is a ninja. Knew it.

"So as I said, when is Marlene going to kick my ass? I want to know. This time I want to at least wear padding before I get knocked down."

He laughed. It was a beautiful sound coming from him. It happened so rarely.

"Marlene has no stake in what I do or don't do, and besides, she's not as violent as Stacy."

I grunted. "What did you ever see in Stacy?"

He glanced at me and thought for a second. "Well, cuddly she's not."

"And you like cuddly." I smiled.

"That I do. But I didn't realize it until I met you."

Aww. My cheeks flamed scarlet. *That was sweet.*

"But to answer your question, she was everything I wasn't. And because of that, she was intriguing at first."

I hung my head. I didn't know if I wanted to hear any more.

"Then I met you. You're every bit as exciting as she is, but you get me. She never did."

I glanced at him. "She never knew about your brother, did she?"

He shook his head.

"You know, she might not have planned the party if she knew."

He nodded.

"So in other words, you never really gave her a chance."

He didn't acknowledge that last statement. He just stood there motionless.

But then it dawned on me. "How did you explain the painting in your office?"

He gave me a confused look. "What do you mean?"

"Didn't she ask about your painting? What did you say?"

"Katie, you are the first person to ask me about the painting."

What? My head just exploded.

"No way. It's front and center in your office!"

"Sometimes the best place to hide something is to put it directly in everyone's face," he stated.

"Or...you put it there because you want someone to notice."

He looked away. "You have a point. But that never happened, until you came along."

I walked over to my couch and motioned Lance to sit next to me. This conversation was taking way too long to continue standing.

"Lance, I have a solution to all of your problems."

He raised his eyebrow at me. "Is that so?"

"Hire old ugly guys. You can't go wrong."

"And you won't get jealous?" He countered.

"Oh, I don't know. They could take one look at you and turn gay. I'm not sure how I would handle that. Cat fights are one thing, but old ugly guys could really take me down. So I might have to fight them off with a stick."

Lance smirked. "You see, that's what I like about you. You have a better image of me than I have of myself. Even though...the thought of old ugly guys chasing after me is disturbing me right now."

I giggled and looked him over from head to toe. *He is really beautiful!*

He took my hand. "Being around you...makes me feel good."

He'd better stop. I might start to cry.

He tilted his head and looked into my eyes. When I noticed, well, I could have just melted. How did he know that his eyes were one of my favorite parts about him? And how did he know how to manipulate me? I wanted to hold on to the anger that I had the other day. But it was so damned hard when he was this close to me.

A phone call wouldn't have worked. That's for sure.

"Katie, it really hurt when you compared me to my father."

My breath hitched. "I know. I'm so sorry for saying that. I have regretted it this whole time."

He shook his head. "But you had a point. I handled the whole situation wrong. But I needed some space to figure things out, and in my mind, you weren't giving it to me."

I looked at our intertwined hands. I had never stopped to try and see things from his point of view. He probably felt like he was caught in a whirlwind.

And a Katie whirlwind could be deadly to mere mortals!

"It felt like you were avoiding me." I whimpered.

"It seemed that way. And I'm sorry for that." His beautiful eyes started to look very sad.

"But when you went to lunch with Stacy instead of me…"

"I didn't know what to do. And I made a bad decision." He sighed. "I was still technically going out with her. What was I supposed to say when she asked me to go to lunch? *Sorry I can't. I need to have lunch with the woman I slept with this weekend. You don't know that I slept with someone else? Oh, my bad.*"

He continued, "Katie, I had to at least try to be fair and break up with her first. I hope you can understand that."

I guess I could. I would want to be treated that way if it was me.

Eep, don't even think about it!

But then that brought up a frosty memory.

"It didn't sound like you broke up with her at lunch." I still held his hand, but I was giving him the harshest frown that I could muster.

"You're right. I was too much of a wimp to tell her."

"Bingo!" I was glad that he finally admitted it.

If he didn't say another word, I thought that I could die in peace after that confirmation.

"I've had a lot of time to think about it since you left. I knew that it was either her or you."

"Well, you made it sound like it was her the last time we talked."

"That's because you were pushing me, and I wanted you to back off."

I didn't answer. I just glared at him.

"So I told her yesterday at work."

"And she was devastated." I assumed.

"Not really."

"Huh?" *What the fuck?*

Then why did she punch me?

"She immediately went up to Led Biggerstaff and started flirting with him."

Yikes! Large and balding? Why go from gorgeous Lance to that gross mess?

But then again, that woman was as smart as a fox.

"That's where she got my address."

Lance looked at me, terror-stricken. "Holy shit! You're probably right."

He cussed. He's not happy. Personnel information is confidential. The boss shouldn't be so easily manipulated.

"Well, your ex is a smart woman. She did have a lot going for her. I hope she doesn't waste it on Biggerstaff."

"Why do you care? She beat you up."

"Only after stealing her boyfriend."

"Yeah, but still. The two of them are cut from the same cloth. They were made for each other."

*Eww...*the thought of Stacy and Led Biggerstaff getting it on made my stomach churn.

Eager to change the subject, I asked, "So what happens now?"

He used his free hand to twirl one of the chestnut curls in my hair around his index finger. "With us? What do you want to happen?"

I furrowed my eyebrows at him. "Are you doing that to get back at me?"

The sensation of his fingers being so close to my neck sent shivers up my spine. I shuddered as he continued to slowly twist my hair, the motion of hair and fingers against the area below my earlobe was both tickling me and turning me on at the same time.

With heavy-lidded eyes, he responded, "Yep. Maybe next time you will just tell me what you want instead of leaving all the decisions up to me."

He's driving me crazy. On purpose.

And when it came to sex, I think I told him exactly what I wanted!

I moaned. "But you were my boss."

He stopped touching my hair and immediately dropped my hand. "I thought I still am."

Whoops. Maybe I still *did* have a job. *Although, I'd much rather continue with the touching!*

"But...aren't you saying that you'd like to have a relationship with me? Perhaps I'm not understanding you. Because, you know, you confuse the hell out of me."

"I'd like to try. I want to see where things go."

"So I shouldn't go back to work."

"Why not?"

This time I looked him in the eyes. "Because I'd rather be with you than have the job."

"We're not getting married, so how will you support yourself?" He looked around my meager surroundings.

Yes, this must be real expensive to maintain.

"We're not getting married?" I asked with feigned surprise.

And when are you going to get back to touching me?

"One step at a time. After all, just a few minutes ago you weren't even talking to me."

But then he couldn't hide the worried expression that crept onto his face. "Now seriously, what are you going to do?"

"I'll manage."

He thought about it for a second. "That's fine. You do what you want. I can get Marlene to come with me on my trips. She's already expressed an interest in the position."

"And what *position* are you referring to?"

He laughed. "Actually, I meant your job. But now that you mention it..."

I squinted at him. "You wouldn't dare."

He shrugged. "A man's gotta do what a man's gotta do. I need an assistant, and my old one just bailed on me."

He had me.

I huffed. "Fine. I'll come back. I know what happens on those trips. I'd probably not feel comfortable with you traveling with someone else, anyway."

He nodded. "Good plan."

"I can see why you're such a good salesperson. But you don't fight fair, Mr. Hardy."

"Mr. Hardy?" He raised an eyebrow at me. "For you, Katie, I will make an exception. You...can call me Lance."

Then he leaned over and hugged me. It was a nice, warm hug.

Wow. I missed feeling him like this. And it had nothing to do with sex. It was his warmth, his gentle demeanor, and his way of caring about those around him.

I knew I never should have said that he doesn't give a shit about anyone else. I knew he did. As a matter of fact, he cared about others much more than he ever cared about himself. And it showed through his actions.

I couldn't stop myself from wanting to be the one he cared about the most.

I then pulled away from the hug so that I could look at him. "We can't do this on a whim."

He shook his head. "Don't worry. I've been thinking about it."

Huh?

"Since when?" I asked.

"Since forever."

Yeah...

"You mean since I walked out of the office?"

His tiny smile appeared. "Something like that."

I shook my head. "What does everyone think about me at work?"

"Do I care?"

I grunted. "Here we go again."

"Don't worry. I'm sure it'll be fine."

"I'm going to feel kinda weird with everyone knowing that I'm sleeping with the boss."

"Wouldn't be the first time in history that's ever happened," he stated.

"But..."

"No buts." He looked toward the door and stood. "I have to get back. I have work to do before tonight. But you probably forgot."

I gave him a confused look. "What did I forget?"

"The conference is at 5:00 p.m. I'm hoping you'll be there."

"What? You have to be kidding. I'm not prepared for that."

He looked at me. "Really, Katie. What did you have to prepare for last time?"

"With this thing?" I pointed to my black eye.

He smiled. "No worries. Just put tons of eye shadow on both eyes. No one will know the difference."

"So I can look like a slut?" I stood and glared at him.

"No." He used his fingers to brush my hair away from my eye and lightly kissed my bruised eyebrow. "Just so that both eyes will match."

How could I say no to him when he was being so sweet?

"I guess I can do that."

He twirled another curl with his finger. "I like your hair this way. Why don't you wear it like this tonight?"

His hand glided against my cheek as he walked out the door.

Breathless. I was totally breathless. And I couldn't move.

Shit! That man has total control over me. I don't know if I like that.

It was sexy for a one night stand, but for a relationship? I'm going to have to find a way to turn the tables, and quick.

⚜

Friday, August 31, 2012 - 3:30 p.m.

I stared at the black eye that was mocking me in the mirror. Lance was completely insane for wanting me to go to the conference looking like this.

I have to wear a ton of eye shadow. Hmm. Well, if my make-up is saying I'm going to a club, then why shouldn't my clothes match?

Lance is usually so calm. Maybe I could do a little something to change that.

I found a short black mini-skirt and a low-cut beaded black top. This outfit was a far cry from the suit I wore for the last conference. Definitely not what a room full of financial advisors would expect. Then again, financial advisors were male for the most part. So they might not even mind.

As a matter of fact, it might even make their evening.

And it did.

I got so many gawking heads turning in my direction that I was afraid that all these strange men might hurt themselves.

Maybe this was a bad idea. This was clearly my *I'm-on-the-prowl* outfit, and it was working too well with all of these slobbering dogs around.

Men *were* dogs. Or pigs. Or...

"Hello, Lance."

His ninja skills must be waning. I felt him sneak up behind me this time.

But what I didn't expect was for him to grab my ass.

I squeaked, but then controlled myself. He was so close behind me that no one could have seen where his hand was.

He is off the hook. What's come over him?

I turned my head and whispered, "If you keep that up, we won't be here long."

He smiled and whispered back, "I just wanted to show you that I noticed. Wasn't that your intention when you decided to dress that way?"

He was still behind me, but from my vantage point, I observed him from top to bottom. He wore his navy blue suit. He looked the same as he had that afternoon. But for some reason, his appearance took my breath away.

That's not fair. He doesn't have to be barely dressed to turn me on. But then again...I can now fantasize about what he looks like underneath that suit!

"That's some outfit," he teased.

"It went with the hair and make-up."

"Mmhmm," he said, as he wrapped his arm around my waist and nuzzled my hair. "And your clothes certainly seem to bring out the best in people."

"Do they bring out the best in you?" I asked.

"What do you think?"

"I don't know. I think you need to show me."

He let go and faced me with his tiny smile. "Later. Let's just get through the next couple of hours."

"Is that a threat or a promise?" I challenged.

"You decide."

Oh Lance...you should know me by now...

"I still don't understand why you need me tonight." People stared at us, but I didn't care.

And of course, Lance didn't either.

"Oh, you will."

Oh hell. The last time he said that was with Dr. Floyd. I definitely wore the wrong outfit...

I'd better look out for horny 90 year olds.

This conference ended up being even easier than the last one was. Lance had to speak only twice. Other than that, he schmoozed with all of the financial advisors. And it seemed that he got even more attention than usual, thanks to my outfit! Take that for strategy.

Is that what he meant? No one seriously hit on me...yet.

It was 9:00, and everyone was gone. Lance walked me out to the main hallway of the convention center. It was sweet. I liked the way he treated me.

I never had a boyfriend who took on the *gentleman* role. I could get quite used to this.

He opened up the main door of the building for me. I watched him. I couldn't get enough of looking at him. But that's how I noticed that his eyes weren't on me.

I followed his eyes and found what he was looking at. There was a white limo parked on the street directly ahead. The driver stood there, and it appeared that he waited for us to arrive.

"Oh, my God. What did you do?"

Chapter 13

Fairy Tale

"What does it look like?" He smiled bigger than usual.

"But why?"

"We never really dated first. I wanted to make it up to you."

I gazed into his eyes. "That wasn't your fault."

"Doesn't matter. Get in." He motioned to the open back door with his arm.

I had never been inside a limo before. The back was big enough to seat six people, and there was a small table in the center of the facing seats that had a bottle of champagne on it.

It was already shaping up to be the best damned date of my life.

I sat down, and Lance sat to my right. I heard the driver close his door, and we took off. But I couldn't see the driver, as a dark window separated the driver from us.

"Where are we going?" I asked.

"My apartment. I have something for you."

"Your big dick?" I flashed him a mischievous grin.

He didn't flinch. "That...and *more*."

"I can hardly wait."

And I couldn't. I kissed along his jaw line. I swear, his jaw was like a magnet to me. I was glad that I got the opportunity to kiss it again.

His fingers ran through my hair, gently holding me close to him. *He really does seem to like my curly hair better!*

I noticed his eyes. They were so gorgeous that I could have drowned in them. I changed course and kissed his lips. They were warm, and I just melted. His lips parted, and our tongues met. *Oh, my God.* His tongue felt like warm velvet, and the sensation of it caused every nerve in my body to tingle.

My body moved on autopilot. Before I knew what I was doing, I was sitting on his lap. My fingers glided through his silky hair, and my other hand fondled him between his legs.

Instead of pushing me away, one hand held me at the base of my neck, and his other arm was around my waist, pulling me closer to him.

I rubbed his manhood, from outside of his pants, until I felt it grow hard. Up and down, I continued to massage his member. All the while, our kiss became more intense. I finally had to break free because I couldn't breathe. But then I saw his eyes again. *Oh God.* I couldn't keep looking at them.

I used the tip of my tongue to trace the outside of his ear. He shuddered a bit, probably from the new sensation coupled with my continued massaging. When I got to his earlobe, I gently nibbled and then...

He grabbed me by the waist and placed me beside him.

What the?

Lance then, painfully, got himself to the driver's window. He knocked, and the window rolled down.

"Yes sir?" the driver asked.

"Will you drive us around for a while? We want to see Manhattan."

I couldn't believe that Lance was able to say that without the heavy breathing.

"No problem, sir." And the dark window rolled back up.

He turned to me and said, "Now, where were we?"

Oh hell. What have I gotten myself into?

He made his way back to me and commanded, "Lie down."

"What?"

His eyes burned with desire. "You took control last time. It's my turn."

His breathing was steady, but I could definitely still hear it.

He guided me to lie down flat on my back. Then he started to undress. The jacket was off and then the tie. But he didn't bother taking off the white shirt. He unbuckled his belt and undid his pants. Those pants were halfway down his thighs when I saw it.

He wore briefs, and the poor things couldn't contain that large an erection.

Luckily they didn't have to, because the briefs were quickly discarded too.

He climbed on top of me, missionary style, and lifted both of my arms over my head. He pinned my wrists with his left hand and used his right to hike up my skirt and slide down my panties. At the same time, he kissed me. He worked his kisses upward starting at my shoulder, then my neck, and finally sucking on the spot right below my earlobe.

He situated the tip of his penis against my vagina and then slid his right hand under my shirt and bra. His fingers massaged my nipple as he captured my mouth in a searing kiss.

Fuck, he's hot.

I pulled away from the kiss and breathlessly said, "Who are you, and what have you done with Lance?"

He smiled. "I've taken him over."

Oh shit, what does that mean?

Well, considering that he was about to enter me, I was about to find out exactly what that meant.

And I liked it.

At first thrust, he did meet with some resistance. But it didn't hurt. It just added to the friction between us. The resistance didn't last long. My body had been longing for him all week, and make-up sex always seemed to be better than usual. He kneaded my breast as he slid in and out of me, and his lips and tongue were back at my neck.

In my life, I had always liked being in control. But somehow, the fact that *he* was doing this to *me,* was getting me more excited than I had anticipated. Normally I would have had my arms around him, but not being able to do that, well, it was an interesting new twist.

All I needed to do was enjoy the ride.

And I did.

My stomach tightened. I didn't know if I was relieved or sad, because what he did to me felt so good. He filled me up, and with every thrust, in and out, he slid against my sensitive spot.

It was warm, it was wet, and it was the closest thing to heaven that I had ever felt.

My thighs shook, and then, an explosion of white light appeared behind my eyelids. I groaned, not wanting to shout Lance's name for fear that the driver might hear me. I could feel my walls squeezing down on Lance's shaft. Just the feeling of it enhanced the sensation of my orgasm and made it last longer.

I felt his body tense, and then a couple of more quick thrusts. I looked at him as his eyelids shut, and then he collapsed on top of me.

He let my wrists go and wrapped both of his arms around me. I intentionally brought my wrists in front of my face and turned my hands. In the heat of passion, he may have held on too tightly. There could be tell-tale marks later...

And that would be fun to explain at the office!

He positioned himself so that his head was below mine. I kissed the top of his head and stroked his silky hair.

At least for the moment, this man was all mine.

What had just happened was quick, wanton sex, and evidently we both needed it. I could feel it in me, and I could feel it *through* him. Of course, it's good when it lasts longer. But apparently we both needed a release.

And we got it.

He held me for a few minutes and then got up and got dressed. He didn't put his tie and jacket back on, but he tried to straighten the rest of his clothing as much as he could.

He was pretty damned wrinkled, and his hair wasn't as perfect as it normally was.

I was just as much of a mess. But I was now thankful that all I had to do was slide my panties back on.

Lance knocked on the driver's window again.

It rolled down to reveal the back of the driver's head.

"Yes sir?"

"We can head home now."

"Okay sir."

I smiled. "He calls you sir."

I had to laugh to myself.

Lance turned to me with an impish grin. "Yeah, but I don't feel like having sex with him afterwards."

"Thank God." But then I blushed. "You don't think he heard us, do you?"

"I don't think he cares. With how much I paid per hour for him and this fancy car, we can do whatever we want to in the back seat of it."

"I see."

Wow. I wondered if this happened all the time to poor limo drivers. I wondered what kind of training prepares them for that.

A few minutes later, the limo pulled up to a tall Manhattan apartment building.

Lance turned to me. "We're here."

I looked up to try and see the top of it. "We're...*here?*"

"Yeah. Come on." He opened the door, got out, and extended his hand to help me.

He was a gentleman. Well, not always. But I really liked it when he decided to be naughty.

He waved at the driver, and the limo pulled away. Lance must have pre-paid.

He held my hand as we walked through the door of his building. We walked past a door man and a security guard standing in the lobby, and he nodded to each. There was a spring to his step that wasn't usually there. Was he proud to be seen with me?

Nah, I'm just feeding my own ego, that's all.

He lived on the 14th floor. We exited the elevator, and he led me to his apartment. It was three doors down on the right.

He opened the door, and I peered in. *Wow, this is nice!* It had windows everywhere, and he had a nice view of the nighttime city skyline.

The living room had hardwood floors and cream-colored furniture. At the center of the room stood a black TV stand, on which was placed a 46-inch flat-screen TV.

His living room was bigger than my whole apartment.

Now that we're in a relationship, I will have to concentrate on bagging this guy. I could definitely get used to living in his world.

He led me to the dining room, and to my surprise, dinner waited on the table.

I turned to him and asked, "How did you do this? You were at the convention. Has this been sitting here the whole time?"

It was a full tray of sushi. That wouldn't be very good after sitting out for so long.

"No. I paid my doorman to let the delivery person in. Since we were later than I expected, it's probably been here for about fifteen minutes." He smiled. "My plan was for it to arrive around the same time we did."

I blushed. "Sorry about that."

He shook his head. "It was worth it."

I surveyed the contents on the table and saw sake sitting beside the sushi.

I pointed to it and said, "That again?"

"Want to try it?"

"I don't really drink. And if I remember correctly, we got in trouble the last time you did."

His tiny smile adorned his lips. "I'm hoping to get into that kind of trouble again."

How do I say no to that?

"Suit yourself. But I want Coke if you have it."

He nodded. But amusement was written all over his face.

My eyes caught sight of his kitchen. It was all stainless steel and granite countertops. But something much more interesting grabbed my attention.

"Oh, my God!" I walked toward the kitchen. "Is that what I think it is?"

I kept walking, and there it was. Sitting on the kitchen counter were two dishes of crème brulee.

He followed me into the kitchen. I looked at him. He had such a smug expression on his face.

"That didn't come from the same restaurant." It wasn't a question on my part but rather an observation.

He nodded.

"Lance, I love you!" I threw my arms around him.

"I know."

I pulled back so that I could see his tiny smile. He was obviously pleased with himself that he had made me so happy. That just made me love him all the more.

"That's for later." He pulled me back to the table.

"Why?" I grabbed in midair.

"Didn't anyone tell you to eat dinner first? That's why I wanted to hide it."

"I always thought that you enjoy the good stuff before it suddenly disappears."

He furrowed his eyebrows at that comment. "Well, I hope that I can change your mind about that."

We sat down and then I admitted, "Lance, you're one of the things that I'm afraid will disappear."

He suddenly froze at my statement. "Katie, let's move past what happened before and enjoy what's happening now."

I shook my head. "It's got nothing to do with this last week. I've just never had anything as good as you in my life before."

"Katie, I *haven't* been very good to you."

"Yes Lance, you have." I took a deep breath. "If tonight qualifies as our first date, then this is the best date I've ever had."

He smiled. "Good. Now eat before we ruin it."

I could hear a soft laugh that he tried to hide.

We quickly devoured the sushi.

I asked him, "Does your mother cook like this?"

His whole face crinkled. "No. Hers is much, much better."

"I wish I could have met her." I was sure I looked a little sad.

"Maybe someday." He glanced at me with those obsidian orbs of his. "If you don't stomp off again."

Two could play at that game. "If you don't tick me off again."

"I'll try not to. But I warned you when we met. Most people don't know how to deal with me."

I looked him straight in the eyes. "But the difference is that I'm willing to try."

He stood and collected the plates. I could tell that what I said meant something to him. But, as usual, his quiet nature didn't allow him to say it.

He came back with the crème brulee and poured some sake for himself and some Coke for me. I dug into the dessert before he even sat back down.

He shook his head at me. "I'm glad you like that so much. I had better stock up."

I stopped eating momentarily to glance at him. "Then I'd never go home, and you wouldn't want that."

"Well, then maybe I'll bring some over to your place."

Yikes! Who would ever want to come to my place when that person lived here?

"No, that's okay. Keep it here."

Then to be clever, I added, "This is so convenient. It's close to the office."

He flashed me an amused smile. "Convenience, huh?"

"Yep, convenience. That's all."

I had been had. I knew it. But I knew that I'd much prefer staying here than ever inviting him to my place.

Then I took a good look at his apartment. There were paintings on the wall. But these weren't images of people. These were landscapes. Even though the art was still very good, it lacked the emotion that I picked up from the previous two pictures I had seen.

"Lance, you painted all these pictures too?" I asked as I pointed each one out.

"You like them?"

"I love your art."

"You want to see my studio?" He stood, his eyes expectant.

He sounded excited, so why not? I let him drag me away from my dessert so that he could show me his studio.

He had a three bedroom apartment. One was the master bedroom, the second a guest room, and the third room was full of his art supplies.

He had a huge blank canvas in one corner, shelves of brushes and paints radiating from it on the adjacent walls, and a lone stool right in the middle.

I turned to him. "Wow. This is amazing. Why didn't you become an artist instead of a broker?"

He smiled as he looked around the room. "I could never pay the bills that way."

"But whatever happened to following your heart?"

"That's what I have you for." He put his arm around my shoulder and gave it a light squeeze.

I scanned the rest of the room, and in the corner opposite from the blank canvas were finished paintings stacked against the wall. All I could see were the back sides of the canvases. It made me curious. I walked away from Lance so that I could see the paintings from the other side.

I flipped each one over. The first one featured a young boy in an oversized football uniform. He was running down the field with the ball in hand.

I looked at Lance, who now stood over me.

"Timmy. He loved sports," he said as he stared at the painting.

Seeing yet another image of this young man made me want to cry.

But that didn't prepare me for the next one. It depicted a very frail image of his brother on a hospital bed. Now the tears sprang to my eyes.

"How did he die?" I couldn't help but ask.

I didn't want to ruin our date, but this picture didn't make it look like a sudden death.

"He died of leukemia at the age of 16."

Oh, my God. He might as well have punched me in the stomach. How tragic.

He put his hand on my shoulder. "Don't cry, Katie. I've already cried enough for both of us."

The picture haunted me. How painful it must have been for Lance to paint it.

Lance then moved his hand from my shoulder to the painting to steady it in my hands. I didn't even know I had started to tremble.

"He was my best friend. Since we moved around a lot due to my dad being in the military, he was the only person that I really got to know."

He took a deep breath. "And then I had to watch him wither away before my very eyes."

I couldn't take it anymore. I flipped to the next picture.

And to my amazement...it was a picture of his mom and dad. They were happy. His tall, red-headed father held his mother in his arms, and they were facing each other and smiling. His mother was absolutely tiny in comparison to his dad.

Wow! His dad was handsome too. Lance got his size and the structure of his face from his dad, but Lance's hair and eyes were all mom's. Lance was slimmer than his dad, but otherwise, it was clear that he had inherited his dad's body. And to think that his dad had to spend his whole life in the military to cultivate his physique, and Lance had pretty much the same while working in the brokerage industry. It almost seemed unfair.

And, judging by the picture, his dad seemed to really love his mom.

I faced Lance. "In this picture, your dad doesn't seem like such a bad guy."

"I never said he was a bad guy. I just said that he didn't give a shit about me."

"But why do you say that?"

He sighed. "Tim was his favorite. Tim was the one who was into sports. I was into art. Dad didn't think that was manly enough."

Shit. What was wrong with his father?

"I was taller than Tim. He was only five-foot-eight. So Dad got Tim into football and tried to get me into basketball. I told him I didn't want to play. Then, when I was offered a scholarship to art school, he didn't want me to take it."

I put the painting down and stood so that I could face him.

"I had just started art school when Tim got sick. I dropped out so that I could be with him."

I can't take much more of this. I thought my story was painful. I guess the grass is always greener on the other side of the fence.

"After Tim died, Dad completely withdrew. So I left for college, majored in Finance, and never went back."

I caressed his cheek and looked deeply into his eyes. There was so much hidden sadness there. I wanted to comfort him and make it all go away. But I didn't know how.

"Lance, do you use your art to work through your emotions? Because when I look at your pictures, I can see so much of you in them."

He looked away from me. "I have something for you."

Then he left the room before I could respond.

He went to his bedroom and came back with a small framed picture.

He placed it in my hands.

It was me.

It was a pencil-sketched picture of my face, my expression a small, vulnerable-looking smile. Even so, I had never looked so beautiful.

"W-what? Why?" I stuttered.

"Wednesday night. I couldn't sleep. I drew this picture of you. As you said, it helped me work through my emotions."

I could only look at the picture of me in silent awe. It was the most romantic gift that I ever could have imagined.

He gently tilted my chin to look back at him.

"Katie, after I saw this picture, I knew what I had to do. I knew that I wanted you back. And I knew that I had to take the necessary steps to get you back."

My fingers trembled. I felt like I was going to cry again. And I had just regained my composure!

I looked back at the picture. It was me. It was the *real* me. How had he been able to capture me like that? How had he been able to see me through the façade that I tried so hard to portray? I always wanted to appear strong, but now I could see that I didn't fool him in the slightest.

Did he like my vulnerable side better?

And, I had obviously not modeled for this picture. How was he able to sketch this from memory? Had he been staring at me as much as I always stared at him?

The thought made my heart flutter.

"You don't like it." He frowned.

That shook me from my thoughts. "I do. Really. I love it!"

I wiped a stray tear from my eye. "It's the best gift I've ever received."

I wrapped my arms around his neck, holding the picture with my hand, and kissed him on the cheek.

He smiled. "I'm glad. I was worried that I upset you."

"You definitely didn't." This time I kissed him on the lips.

When we parted, he motioned me back toward the dining room. "Do you want to finish your dessert now?"

"If you don't mind, I'm interested in a different type of dessert." I took him by the hand and led him to the bedroom instead.

He didn't seem to mind.

He had a huge king-sized bed. Well, maybe it was bigger than king-sized, if that was even possible. It was covered with an ebony silk bed cover, and when I sat down on it, it felt like the mattress conformed to me. I gently placed my picture on his night table.

He sat down beside me and wrapped his arms around my waist. Then he nuzzled his head against my shoulders and lightly placed his lips against my collar bone.

I melted at first, but then I tried to snap out of it. "Hey, this time *you* need to lie down!"

"No. I'm still making up for the first time you attacked me."

"Oh, no you don't." I playfully pushed him down on the bed.

"I don't intend to just lie here this time," he said dryly.

"Hmm." I looked around. "Fine. How about you do me while I do you."

"What?" He looked confused.

"You'll see."

I decided to do my own strip tease, like he had done in the limo. But mine was going to be a bit slower and more demonstrative.

I grabbed the hem of my shirt and pulled it over my head, exposing the black lace bra underneath. I congratulated myself on having had the foresight to wear the sexy bra.

I leaned toward him, chest forward. "Do you like what you see?"

"What do you think?" He sat up and placed his hand on my breast and tried to kiss my neck.

I pulled away. "No. Not yet."

I slid my black mini-skirt down my legs to reveal the matching black lace panties.

I rubbed my hands from my butt to my thighs. "Is this what you want?"

He frowned. "Yeah, but it's taking too long."

I laughed. "Good things come to those who wait."

He started to get off the bed, but I pushed him back down. "Okay. Okay."

I climbed on top of him. He sat on the edge of the bed, and I sat on his lap, straddling him.

One-by-one, I undid all of the buttons on his shirt. I nibbled on his earlobe as I slid it off his shoulders.

He hooked his fingers onto my bra straps and slowly pulled them down. His fingers left a warm trail as they went.

My breasts were now exposed, and he took a nipple in his mouth. As he did, I could feel the charge throughout my body, and the area between my legs ached for him.

I could feel his tongue swirl around, and his lips massaged the sensitive area. I almost did not realize that his hands were unhooking my bra.

The garment was discarded, and I was sinking fast. I could feel his erection press up against me, and it would have been very easy to end things right there. But I was determined. I had something else in mind.

"Lance," I said breathlessly. "Lie down."

He lifted his head momentarily. "Why?"

His face was so incredibly sexy at that moment that I almost lost my nerve. But then I pushed him down on the bed.

"You'll see." I barely breathed out.

I unbuttoned his pants and pulled them off of his legs. There was his erection again. I then pulled off his briefs.

I slid my own panties off and climbed on top of him, but this time in the opposite direction. My bare breasts were pressed up against his abdomen, my private area dangerously close to his face.

I took his shaft in my hand and dipped the head of it into my mouth. My lips massaged the edge of the crown. I was getting into it until I discovered that he picked up on the idea. His hands were on my hips, and he positioned me so that he could participate. The next thing I felt was his tongue swirl around my clit.

Oh God. My whole body responded to what he was doing to me. *This was my idea? How could I possibly concentrate on getting him off when I enjoyed what he was doing so much?*

My responses toward him became more urgent. I used the tip of my tongue to trace the seam underneath his swollen crown. I took his head into my mouth and then let go so that I could lick him up and down, from the hole at the tip back down to the center below his head. I soon surrounded his entire head with my tongue. Or at least I tried, due to the size of the thing. Judging by his moans, he seemed to be enjoying it.

All the while, the tip of his tongue had been circling my clit. Then he took my inner lips into his mouth, applying a modest amount of pressure while rolling his tongue in and out of the crevice. And then he stuck his tongue deep into my hole.

I screamed out and almost exploded.

I couldn't stand it anymore. I rolled off of him and positioned myself directly over his hard dick. He was going to get it, and I was going to give it to him right now.

I plunged it right inside of me. I let out a heavy sigh. He filled me up, and my whole body reverberated with a sense of pleasure that conquered all of my senses.

It didn't take long. I rose up and down on him, and the sensitive area inside of me craved him. With every movement, I could feel the tension rise within me. I couldn't breathe. As his shaft slid in and out of me, my vibrations took control.

And then I felt it, my walls clamped down on him, and this time, I felt him pulse inside of me at the same time. My body jerked in all directions, and I couldn't have stopped it if I tried.

I was descending from my high when I looked at Lance. His head was turned to the side, and he breathed heavily.

His face, that porcelain-looking skin, and that black hair. He was so perfect. Even in the heat of passion, I couldn't take my eyes off of him.

I pulled myself up and rolled over to his side. I lay on top of his arm, and his hand settled itself on my hip. My arm was around his waist, and my ear lay against his chest.

His heartbeat soothed me. It beat hard at the moment, but hearing and feeling the rhythm of it helped me to calm my own heart.

Through our embrace, I could feel his warmth again. And I was drowning in it. What I was feeling was not a panicked type of sensation. Instead it was extremely calming.

Here I was, holding this man again like I had the first night we slept together. And I loved it. The feelings that I got from cuddling with him were a very close second to actually making love to him. In his arms, I felt protected. I felt loved. I felt connected.

I could get used to sleeping this way for the rest of my life.

And that is precisely what I planned to do.

Whether Lance knew it or not.